EMMA'S WAR

Book One
GOODBYE DAD

DEDICATION

Dedicated to my grandchildren
— K. H. I. and J.
and to 'Bill,' 'Fran' and 'Jonty'
with many thanks for their shared memories

BY THE SAME AUTHOR

Book One

Goodbye Dad!

VIOLET BRAND

EGON PUBLISHERS LTD

Published in 1991
Reprinted 1992
by Egon Publishers Ltd,
Royston Road, Baldock, Herts SG7 6NW

ISBN 0 905858 58 1

Illustrations by Tony Richards

Designed and printed in Great Britain by
Streetsprinters,
Royston Road, Baldock,
Herts SG7 6NW

Contents

INTRODUCTION

VIOLET BRAND was ten years old when the war broke out. She lived in Canterbury, Kent and vividly remembers the Battle of Britain fought overhead during the summer of 1940, then the sudden evacuation of children in September, due to an invasion scare.

She and her family returned to Canterbury, after four months in Reading and, like many others, were there during the Blitz on June 1st, 1942. Her own school was destroyed that night and the school of her younger brother and sister was damaged by incendiary bombs.

The air raid siren, Tug-Boat Annie (the noise which issued forth to tell them that enemy planes were overhead) and air raid shelters, were part of everyday life, as were the tragedies that struck the families of friends. Barrage balloons and the havoc they could cause will never be forgotten.

The final years of the war brought other experiences and inevitably, nothing could separate those which were part of a teenager's life within the family and those which were the direct result of the Second World War.

She says that between 1939 and 1945 she was often very scared, but never bored. It was impossible to know what the next day would bring.

She was one of a family of four children and it is on their experiences that 'Emma's War' is based. Canterbury and Kenabury, home of 'Emma's' family, have much in common. The Dane John park with its burial mound and the lofty cathedral which remained almost untouched, despite the destruction of many surrounding buildings, are as much part of Canterbury today, as they were of the 'Kenabury' where 'Emma' lived during the war.

The social conditions which were common to all working-class families, would have been the same irrespective of the war — and the strong community spirit always exisited.

Violet Brand has manipulated some dates, places, events and people to ensure that the effects of the war on one family growing up between 1939–45, will be meaningful to children growing up in the 1990s — including her own grandchildren.

Chapter One

YOU'VE GOT TO GO

'Coo, look at that,' said Bill, as the plane twisted and turned out of the sky, smoke belching from its tail.

'Look. The pilot's baling out,' said Jimmy excitedly.

'They're going to land in the orchards,' said Bill and he jumped up from his stool, knocking over his basket of hops as he did so.

'Bill, now look what you've done,' protested Mum. 'Pick them up.'

Jimmy in the next row smothered a laugh. His fingers slowly felt for the hops on the bine across his knees, whilst his eyes were on the sky. Suddenly, he was on his feet.

'Can we go?' he asked his mother. '*Please*, Mum.'

Mrs Turner bent round to see Mrs Barton between the hop poles.

'Shall we let them?' she asked. 'They're not going to do much good here if we don't.'

Mum saw the point. 'All right, Bill,' she said. 'You can go.' Without further talk, the two boys dashed up the earthy tracks between the rows of hop poles to grab their bikes.

'It's not fair,' pouted Emma. 'Why can the boys *always* go off to do something exciting, whilst girls have to sit picking boring old hops, getting black and scratched.'

'Wish I was a boy,' grumbled Betty Turner from the row next door.

'Well you're not,' said Mrs Turner firmly, 'so you'll have to put up with it.'

The planes were still scrapping overhead, the white streaks from their tails crossing and uncrossing, as they wove in and out of each other. Their guns spattered on and the hop-pickers could see little spots of smoke in the clear blue sky.

It had been the most exciting hop-picking that Emma could ever remember. Usually, it was a mixture of fun, work and dirt, with a little extra pocket-money in September, when Mum was paid. Most of the money went on clothes — new shoes and coats always had to wait until the 'oppin' money was collected.

But this year, the siren* had gone almost every day and the planes had been fighting overhead.

'If we'd been at school,' thought Emma, 'we would have missed seeing all of this.'

All through the holidays, if the boys thought that there was any chance of getting to a shot down plane before the police, or soldiers, they were on their bikes, and away. Sometimes, they came back with a small piece of a plane. If it had a sign, or a number painted on it, then that was very valuable indeed. Bill had quite a few of these pieces in his bedroom.

Betty declared that Jimmy had a pile as well.

'Tall-ee,' came the shout at the end of the row. The big man was already there, with string hanging from his belt and a big, empty sack over his arm. He dragged behind him another huge sack, half full of hops.

Mum gently, very gently, tipped the hops the Barts had picked into the huge tally basket, taking care not to let them sink. By this time Mr Wells the tally man had hobbled along, with the tally sticks rattling on the string round his waist.

'Nearly full, Mrs Bart,' he said. 'You'll need about another 'alf bushel.'

Mum turned and called out.

'We need yours. Emma. Bring them up quickly.'

Finally, the huge basket was full and the hops were emptied into the giant sack. Mr Wells marked Mum's tally stick.

'Where's your boy?' he asked.

'Gone to try and get a bit of that plane that came down,' Mum replied.

'Hm,' snorted Mr Wells. 'The Guv'ner says all the kids are going to be evacuated in the next few days.'

Mum looked stunned.

*air raid warning

'What, sent away?' she asked in a startled voice. Emma crept nearer to hear. She was frightened.

'Yep,' replied Mr Wells. 'They think there's going to be an invasion.' He hobbled away, not looking again at the concerned faces he was leaving behind.

Mum and Emma went back down the row. Mrs Turner called out.

'You were lucky, Bart, to have enough for a tally. We must be slowing up.' She laughed.

Mum went over to her and Emma crawled through the empty bines towards Betty, who was still picking away.

'Did you hear what Mr Wells said?' asked Emma in a quiet voice, as she crouched down beside Betty's stool.

'No,' replied Betty. 'He never says anything very important — or funny, so I don't listen.'

'Well *this was* important,' said Emma. 'Mr Cooper says that we are all going to be sent away, because they think there'll be an invasion.'

Betty looked surprised.

'How *can* Mr *Cooper* know that?' she asked, not wanting to believe what she heard.

'Well,' said Emma. 'He's a boss — and bosses are important — so I suppose people tell him things.'

'When does he think we've got to go?' asked Betty, beginning to look anxious.

'Soon — this week,' said Emma.

'But they can't do that,' said Betty. 'Where will they send us? Can they *make* us go?'

'Dunno,' said Emma. 'Let's see what the Mums are saying.'

Betty got up from her stool and the girls walked to where their mothers were quietly talking.

'You've told Betty then,' said Mum.

'Yes,' said Emma, 'but do you really think it's true?'

'Not sure,' was the reply.

'Tell you what,' said Mrs Turner. 'When the boys come back, let them go into the town to see what they can discover.'

'Sounds a good idea,' said Mum.

'Why can't *we* go?' pleaded Emma.

'The boys can go on their bikes,' said Mum. 'Be quicker.'

'Let's do some picking,' said Mrs Turner. 'If all you kids disappear, Mr Cooper's hops won't be picked 'til October!'

'No hops — no beer,' laughed Mum.

'Hops, hops, hops,' moaned Betty, as they sat on their stools, bines on their laps and went on picking. Their fingers were going slowly. There was so much to think about — to worry about.

Fran came rushing up 'Mum,' she shouted. 'Moggy's coming round with her barrow. Can we go and get some sweets?'

'No,' said Mum firmly. 'You know what I think of Moggy's sweets. The cats sleep all over them.'

Jonty was close behind Fran and his little face crumpled with disappointment.

'Just one,' he pleaded.

'No — *none* of them are clean,' said Mum.

In the next alley. Mrs Turner was having the same argument with her little ones. Fortunately, a bell could be heard in the distance, followed by a voice shouting,

'Wall-zee, Wall-zee.'*

'The Wallzee man,' said Fran excitedly. *'He's* clean. Can we have one?'

---

*fruit water ice made by Wall's Ice-cream

'Yes,' relented Mum. 'Here's a penny.' she fished it out of her apron pocket. 'Get two. We'll cut them in halves and you can share them.'

'Not one each?' Fran looked disappointed.

'Sorry, no,' said Mum, 'You can share that penny. It's all I've got — so it's half a Wallzee — or nothing.'

Fran took the penny and she and Jonty ran off. As they disappeared round the hop poles, two clouds of dust came towards the pickers. Brakes squealed and Jimmy and Bill fell off their bikes, so eager to give their news, that they could not wait to get off properly.

'We've got to go,' said Bill.

'Tomorrow,' said Jimmy.

'What do you mean?' asked Mum.

'On our way back from the orchard,' explained Bill, 'We met Mr King.'

'He stopped us,' went on Jimmy, 'and we wondered what we'd done wrong.'

'No — really, he was very kind,' said Bill. 'Asked us if we'd been into the town to see the notices.'

'What notices?' asked Mrs Turner.

'The notices say that *all* mothers and children have got to get out of the city by tomorrow,' said Jimmy.

'By tomorrow?' Mum looked shattered.

'Yes, we've got to be evacuated,' put in Bill.

'But where are we supposed to go?' Mrs Turner looked stumped for a solution.

'And how are we supposed to get there?' asked Mum.

'Well,' went on Bill, 'the older children are supposed to go away with their schools and the younger ones, the under fives, go with their mothers.'

'But where to?' Mum insisted.

'Nobody seems to know — not even Mr King,' said Bill.

14

the Head Master's house. A few teachers were
answering questions.
…oys propped their bikes against a wall and ran over
…one of the groups. Betty and Emma stood back.
…what their notices say first,' said Emma, still
…t to show her scruffy self in the Girls' School. The
…me back to them.
…o be at the West station tomorrow morning at eight
…' said Bill.
…arly,' stammered Emma.
…ve got to take one bag with clothes, ration book and
…sk,' said Jimmy.
…es, and enough food for the journey,' added Bill.
…n what?' asked Betty.
…get on trains and go away,' said Jimmy, shrugging
…ulders.
…— where to?' Emma was puzzled.
…no,' said Bill. 'It doesn't say.'
…we all go on the same train to the same place?' asked

…no,' said Jimmy. 'Doesn't say.'
…s go and look on *my* notices,' said Emma. 'See if it
…e same.'
…y walked along the path to the Head Mistress's
…One again, notices were pinned up and girls were
…ng round reading them.
…on, Em,' said Bill. 'Get in there and see what it

…ctantly, Emma went towards the smallest group. All
…girls seemed so clean! She stood at the back, trying
…, but the notice was too far away and the writing was
…all.
…o are *you*?' asked a clear voice above her.
…ma looked up and vaguely recognised one of the

'What did he say we should do, then?' Mum wanted to know.

'Well, he said that Emma and me, and Jimmy and Betty, had better go to our schools this afternoon to find out,' replied Bill.

Emma could not believe that all this was happening so quickly. It was only a few minutes ago that Mr Wells had even mentioned evacuation and invasion.

One thing she *did* know, she did *not* want to go to her school, especially in her dirty, scruffy, hop-picking clothes.

'I don't *know* anyone,' she thought, beginning to wish she had not passed the scholarship to Blankton Girls' School.

'I only wish I was going to Chanters with Betty and all our other friends,' she thought. It was all right for Jimmy and Bill. They went to the same school.

'The girls had better go with the boys then,' said Mum.

'Yes,' agreed Mrs Turner. 'Take off your aprons — and off you go.'

'Come back here,' said Mum, 'as long as it's before five — otherwise go straight home.'

'Can't we go home and get cleaned up first?' pleaded Emma.

'Better not,' said Mum, 'cos that'll take a lot of time.'

The boys picked up their bikes and the four of them trudged up the earthy tracks between the hop poles.

'Don't feel very happy about this,' murmered Betty to Emma.

'Nor me,' agreed Emma. 'And I *hate* having to go to Blankton looking like this.'

'Hope you don't meet any of the posh ones,' said Betty, sympathetically.

15

The little ones were coming towards them, clutching the paper-wrapped Wallzees.

Fran asked, 'Aren't you staying to eat yours?'

'Can't,' said Emma. 'Got to go into the town. Can't go back and cut it.'

'Good-ee,' said Fran. 'Jonty and me can have a whole one each! They'll have melted before you get back.'

The pair of them ran excitedly towards Mum.

'The boys and the little ones are having all the fun this afternoon,' said Emma.

'Not fair, is it?' agreed Betty.

Chapter Two

THE DIRTY NEW GIRL

'WHERE shall we go first?' called Bill, bikes in a zig-zag fashion through avenue.

'Blankton,' Emma called back. ' Then we can all go with Betty to C

The boys seemed satisfied and ride, just missing each other, as they planes in the sky.

'Do you mind?' Emma asked Bett don't have to go there alone.'

'I don't mind,' said Betty, 'as long after.'

As they approached the rear gates looked up at the high wall beside th twenty cats sat on it — black, tabby

'Moggy's cats,' she laughed. ' 'spect she's in the hop-fields.'

'What a scraggy lot they are,' said I she feeds them?'

'No, only on mice and sweets,' laug

They walked into Blankton Boys' groups standing around notices tha

outside
nearby

The b
to join

'See
reluctar
boys ca

'Got
o'clock.

'So e

'You'

gas ma

'Oh

'The

'We
his sho

'But

'Dur

'Do
Betty.

'Dur

'Let'
says th

The
house.
crowdi

'Go
says.'

Rel
of the
to rea
too sn

'Wh
Em

teachers she had met when she came for her interview.

'I – I'm a new girl,' stammered Emma.

'Yes,' said the clear, precise voice. 'Rather a *dirty* new girl. I hope you will be somewhat cleaner when you come to *this* school.'

Emma's cheeks went bright scarlet and she was aware of pairs and pairs of eyes staring at her. She wished she could run away.

'It's 'oppin', Miss,' she stammered out.

'*What's h*opping?' asked the haughty voice.

'I mean – I mean, it's hop-picking time and I came straight here, Miss,' said Emma.

'My *name*,' said the voice, 'is Miss Pring. Do *not* forget that.'

'No Miss Pring. Yes Miss Pring,' gabbled Emma, just wishing she was going to *any other* school but Blankton.

'Now read the notice and then ask any questions.' With that, Miss Pring turned away to speak to one of the other girls.

A tall, ginger-haired girl took Emma's hand.

'Come on — through here,' she said. 'Don't take any notice of Pringle. We all *hate* her,' she whispered.

Emma's eyes were so full of tears that she could not even *see* the notice. She lifted her black, hoppy hand to her eyes to brush them away. The tall ginger-haired girl said, 'Here, use my hanky. I used to go hoppin',' so I know what it's like.' She looked so clean, that Emma could hardly believe it.

'I go apple-picking now. Much cleaner,' the ginger-haired girl went on. 'Once you've taken off your apron and changed your shoes, you look quite respectable. Better paid too!'

Emma took the clean hanky and wiped her eyes. She read the notice.

EVACUATION

All city girls are to be evacuated tomorrow.

Meet at the West Station at 8 a.m. in **school uniform** (winter) with a change of clothing, plus night clothes, in a bag, or case.

Please bring coats as it is not known for how long you will be away.

Bring ration books, food for one day and **gas-masks.**

Younger sisters may accompany Blankton girls, even though they may attend another city school.

Country girls are not being evacuated at this time. Normal school will resume for them as soon as possible.

**Miss Evelyn Cannon
Head Mistress**

'Are *you* going?' Emma asked the ginger-haired girl.

'Yes — got to,' replied the older girl. 'I'll look out for you.'

'Thanks,' said Emma gratefully. 'I don't *know* anybody, so it's awful.'

'Must be,' said the girl. 'It's bad enough for us who've been here a few years, but for new girls — it's terrible.'

'It says I can bring my younger sister,' said Emma. 'Is that right?'

'Well, it says so,' said the the big girl. 'Tell you what, come with me and we'll ask Miss Plath. She's *really* nice and friendly.'

They moved away from the group of girls and walked past Bill, Jimmy and Betty on their way to see Miss Plath.

'I'm just going to find out about Fran,' said Emma hurriedly. 'That's my brother and some friends,' she explained.

'What did he say we should do, then?' Mum wanted to know.

'Well, he said that Emma and me, and Jimmy and Betty, had better go to our schools this afternoon to find out,' replied Bill.

Emma could not believe that all this was happening so quickly. It was only a few minutes ago that Mr Wells had even mentioned evacuation and invasion.

One thing she *did* know, she did *not* want to go to her school, especially in her dirty, scruffy, hop-picking clothes.

'I don't *know* anyone,' she thought, beginning to wish she had not passed the scholarship to Blankton Girls' School.

'I only wish I was going to Chanters with Betty and all our other friends,' she thought. It was all right for Jimmy and Bill. They went to the same school.

'The girls had better go with the boys then,' said Mum.

'Yes,' agreed Mrs Turner. 'Take off your aprons — and off you go.'

'Come back here,' said Mum, 'as long as it's before five — otherwise go straight home.'

'Can't we go home and get cleaned up first?' pleaded Emma.

'Better not,' said Mum, 'cos that'll take a lot of time.'

The boys picked up their bikes and the four of them trudged up the earthy tracks between the hop poles.

'Don't feel very happy about this,' murmered Betty to Emma.

'Nor me,' agreed Emma. 'And I *hate* having to go to Blankton looking like this.'

'Hope you don't meet any of the posh ones,' said Betty, sympathetically.

The little ones were coming towards them, clutching the paper-wrapped Wallzees.

Fran asked, 'Aren't you staying to eat yours?'

'Can't,' said Emma. 'Got to go into the town. Can't go back and cut it.'

'Good-ee,' said Fran. 'Jonty and me can have a whole one each! They'll have melted before you get back.'

The pair of them ran excitedly towards Mum.

'The boys and the little ones are having all the fun this afternoon,' said Emma.

'Not fair, is it?' agreed Betty.

Chapter Two

THE DIRTY NEW GIRL

'Where shall we go first?' called Bill, as the boys rode their bikes in a zig-zag fashion through the wide Dane John avenue.

'Blankton,' Emma called back. 'That'll be three of us. Then we can all go with Betty to Chanters.'

The boys seemed satisfied and continued their crazy ride, just missing each other, as they wove around like the planes in the sky.

'Do you mind?' Emma asked Betty. 'I'll feel better if I don't have to go there alone.'

'I don't mind,' said Betty, 'as long as you come with me after.'

As they approached the rear gates of the school, Emma looked up at the high wall beside the pavement. About twenty cats sat on it — black, tabby, ginger, all sorts.

'Moggy's cats,' she laughed. ' 'spect they're shut out, 'cos she's in the hop-fields.'

'What a scraggy lot they are,' said Betty. 'Do you think she feeds them?'

'No, only on mice and sweets,' laughed Emma.

They walked into Blankton Boys' playground and saw groups standing around notices that were pinned up

outside the Head Master's house. A few teachers were nearby answering questions.

The boys propped their bikes against a wall and ran over to join one of the groups. Betty and Emma stood back.

'See what their notices say first,' said Emma, still reluctant to show her scruffy self in the Girls' School. The boys came back to them.

'Got to be at the West station tomorrow morning at eight o'clock,' said Bill.

'So early,' stammered Emma.

'You've got to take one bag with clothes, ration book and gas mask,' said Jimmy.

'Oh yes, and enough food for the journey,' added Bill.

'Then what?' asked Betty.

'We get on trains and go away,' said Jimmy, shrugging his shoulders.

'But — where to?' Emma was puzzled.

'Dunno,' said Bill. 'It doesn't say.'

'Do we all go on the same train to the same place?' asked Betty.

'Dunno,' said Jimmy. 'Doesn't say.'

'Let's go and look on *my* notices,' said Emma. 'See if it says the same.'

They walked along the path to the Head Mistress's house. One again, notices were pinned up and girls were crowding round reading them.

'Go on, Em,' said Bill. 'Get in there and see what it says.'

Reluctantly, Emma went towards the smallest group. All of the girls seemed so clean! She stood at the back, trying to read, but the notice was too far away and the writing was too small.

'*Who* are *you*?' asked a clear voice above her.

Emma looked up and vaguely recognised one of the

teachers she had met when she came for her interview.

'I–I'm a new girl,' stammered Emma.

'Yes,' said the clear, precise voice. 'Rather a *dirty* new girl. I hope you will be somewhat cleaner when you come to *this* school.'

Emma's cheeks went bright scarlet and she was aware of pairs and pairs of eyes staring at her. She wished she could run away.

'It's 'oppin', Miss,' she stammered out.

'*What's h*opping?' asked the haughty voice.

'I mean–I mean, it's hop-picking time and I came straight here, Miss,' said Emma.

'My *name*,' said the voice, 'is Miss Pring. Do *not* forget that.'

'No Miss Pring. Yes Miss Pring,' gabbled Emma, just wishing she was going to *any other* school but Blankton.

'Now read the notice and then ask any questions.' With that, Miss Pring turned away to speak to one of the other girls.

A tall, ginger-haired girl took Emma's hand.

'Come on — through here,' she said. 'Don't take any notice of Pringle. We all *hate* her,' she whispered.

Emma's eyes were so full of tears that she could not even *see* the notice. She lifted her black, hoppy hand to her eyes to brush them away. The tall ginger-haired girl said, 'Here, use my hanky. I used to go hoppin',' so I know what it's like.' She looked so clean, that Emma could hardly believe it.

'I go apple-picking now. Much cleaner,' the ginger-haired girl went on. 'Once you've taken off your apron and changed your shoes, you look quite respectable. Better paid too!'

Emma took the clean hanky and wiped her eyes. She read the notice.

EVACUATION

All city girls are to be evacuated tomorrow.

Meet at the West Station at 8 a.m. in **school uniform** (winter) with a change of clothing, plus night clothes, in a bag, or case.

Please bring coats as it is not known for how long you will be away.

Bring ration books, food for one day and **gasmasks.**

Younger sisters may accompany Blankton girls, even though they may attend another city school.

Country girls are not being evacuated at this time. Normal school will resume for them as soon as possible.

Miss Evelyn Cannon
Head Mistress

'Are *you* going?' Emma asked the ginger-haired girl.

'Yes — got to,' replied the older girl. 'I'll look out for you.'

'Thanks,' said Emma gratefully. 'I don't *know* anybody, so it's awful.'

'Must be,' said the girl. 'It's bad enough for us who've been here a few years, but for new girls — it's terrible.'

'It says I can bring my younger sister,' said Emma. 'Is that right?'

'Well, it says so,' said the the big girl. 'Tell you what, come with me and we'll ask Miss Plath. She's *really* nice and friendly.'

They moved away from the group of girls and walked past Bill, Jimmy and Betty on their way to see Miss Plath.

'I'm just going to find out about Fran,' said Emma hurriedly. 'That's my brother and some friends,' she explained.

'Nice of them to come with you,' said the big girl. 'What's your name?'

'Emma,' was the reply. 'What's yours?'

'Mary,' the ginger-haired girl replied.

They approached a tall, slim lady with steel-grey hair, swept back into a bun.

'Please, Miss Plath, can you help?' Mary asked.

Miss Plath turned towards them and smiled, a very friendly smile.

'Good afternoon, Mary,' she said. 'Who is your young friend?'

'This is Emma,' replied Mary. 'She's new, but she'll be coming away with us.'

Miss Plath looked down at Emma. 'In the middle of hop-picking too!' she said. 'The farmers won't be very pleased.' She sounded as if she *knew* about hop-picking and certainly did not make Emma feel scruffy and dirty.

'It's my younger sister,' said Emma shyly. 'It says on the notice that our sisters can come with us, even though they go to another school. Is that right?'

'How old is your sister, Emma?' asked Miss Plath.

'She's eight,' replied Emma.

'Oh yes,' said Miss Plath. 'She can come and be billetted with you.'

'You mean — stay in the same house?' asked Emma.

'That's it,' replied Miss Plath. 'You'll like that, I'm sure, especially if you don't know many girls here. It'll be nice to have someone from the same family with you.'

'Oh yes,' agreed Emma, feeling relieved. 'Very nice.'

'Are there any more of you?' Miss Plath asked.

'Well, there's my older brother,' replied Emma. 'He's at Blankton Boys, so he'll go with them. That's him, standing across there with some friends.'

'You've all been hopping together I see,' said Miss Plath. 'I bet it's fun.'

'Yes, it is,' agreed Emma, delighted to know that at least *one* teacher was being kind and understanding.

'Then, there's my little brother,' said Emma. 'He's only four.'

'Your mother will have to go away with him,' Miss Plath told her. 'She should come to the West Station at eight o'clock tomorrow, ready to get on the train.'

'Where are the trains going?' asked Mary.

'I really don't know,' replied Miss Plath.

'Are we all going to the same place?' asked Emma.

'We don't know that either,' said Miss Plath. 'It's all happened so quickly, that we really don't know any more than is on the notices.'

'Are *you* coming?' Emma asked timidly.

'Yes, I'm coming,' Miss Plath assured her.

'I'm glad,' said Emma with a sigh of relief.

'So am I,' said Mary, 'and I've been here for years and know lots of people.'

'It's hard this happening when you're just starting with us,' said Miss Plath, 'but you'll soon make friends.'

More girls were beginning to come up to ask questions and she turned to go.

'See you tomorrow,' she said.

'Thank you, Mary,' said Emma. 'It was really nice of you to help me.'

'That's O.K.,' said Mary. 'See you at the West Station tomorrow. 'Bye.'

''Bye,' said Emma and went back to the others.

'What on earth was all that about?' asked Bill.

'Well, it was about Fran,' replied Emma. 'She can come with me, but Mum will have to go away with Jonty.'

'Poor Dad,' said Bill. 'He'll be all alone.'

' 'spect that's what they want,' said Jimmy. 'Just men to fight — or whatever.'

'Dad fighting!' thought Emma. 'He's *not* a soldier, just a fireman. He's too old to join up.'

She did not say anything aloud, because Betty was anxious to be off to Chanters and read *her* notices. The boys collected their bikes and they all walked through the groups of girls, out of the front entrance into the High Street.

'It all looks normal,' said Emma, as mothers hustled in and out of shops with their loaded shopping baskets. Babies cried in prams and toddlers trailed behind.

'What will it be like tomorrow?' asked Betty.

'Empty,' replied Emma. 'The shops will be empty.'

'Can't imagine the High Street without people,' said Betty.

'On Saturdays it'll be full of men stocking up for the week,' said Emma.

The boys were pushing their bikes ahead of them.

'We'll ride on,' called Jimmy.

'See you at Chanters,' shouted Bill. They jumped on their bikes and rode off.

'One of those teachers was *really* nasty,' said Emma.

'We heard her,' said Betty. 'Toffee-nosed woman!'

'Still,' went on Emma, 'Miss Plath's nice and Mary, the ginger-haired girl, is *really* friendly.'

They had reached the cattle market at the top of the town. A few remaining sheep were baa-ing in their pens and six cows were being pushed into the auctioneer's ring. The farmers crowded round, pipes in mouths, eyeing the black and white cows up and down.

'What am I bid?' the auctioneer shouted.

After that, his voice moved so fast that Emma could not understand a word he said, until the end. Then — 'Going,

23

going, gone' and he banged his wooden gavel* onto the table.

'Will they still hold markets if there's an invasion?' Betty wondered.

'Dunno. We won't be here to find out,' was Emma's dismal reply.

'Come on, cheer up,' said Betty. 'We won't be away for long.'

'Hope not,' said Emma, and really meant it.

They soon arrived at Chanters School and went in through the gate to the girls' playground.

'Hi,' said girl after girl.

'What are *you* doing here?' asked one. 'You belong with the snobby Blankers now.' The others laughed and Emma felt uncomfortable.

Betty replied, 'Emma's my friend *whatever* school she goes to,' and tucked her arm through Emma's.

Emma was feeling thoroughly miserable.

'Wish I hadn't won that jolly old scholarship,' she muttered. 'I was happy at the other school — *really* happy with lots of friends.'

'You'll soon have lots of friends again,' Betty assured her. 'But don't forget me — I'm your *best* friend.'

'Yes,' agreed Emma gratefully. 'You *are* my best friend.'

Betty went up to read the notice. Emma saw it too. It was exactly the same as the Blankton notice, apart from the name at the bottom and the bit about country girls. Country girls did not go Chanters.

'You can take Babs with you then,' Emma said. 'That'll be nice.'

'S'pose it will,' said Betty, slightly reluctantly. 'I think I might rather go on my own. I've got lots of friends here and

*small wooden hammer

24

my young sister's a bit of a cry-baby, you know. Not sure how I'd cope.'

Emma nodded. She understood. Fran was the giggler and Babs the whiner. At this time, she was so very glad about that.

'Ask your Mum,' she said. 'Let her decide.'

Betty chatted to a few girls, whilst Emma went across to the gate to join the boys.

'Bet you wish you were at Chanters, don't you?' teased Bill.

'Shut up,' said Emma crossly, because that is exactly what she *did* wish. It was all right for Bill and Jimmy. They had *both* won scholarships to the Boys' School and they were not even 'best' friends.

'Boys don't really have "best" friends,' thought Emma. 'They go around in gangs, but girls *need* someone special.'

The boys had propped their bikes against the wall and were having a friendly scrap. Betty came back.

'Better get back to our Mums,' she said. 'It's half past three *now*. Not much time to sort out everything by eight o'clock tomorrow morning.'

'Heavens no!' said Emma. 'Come on boys — we'd better go.'

'We'll ride on,' they said and hopped on their bikes.

By the time the girls had arrived back, the boys had told the latest news. Mum and Mrs Turner were hurriedly emptying the remaining hops into the tally basket. Mr Wells hobbled from one anxious hop-picker to another, grumbling.

'Dunno 'ow we're gonner ge' this lot in — no pickers — flippin' war.'

Mum did not have a full tally again, so he handed her tokens for three and a half bushels.

'Won't see *you* again then, Mrs Bart?' he asked.

'No,' replied Mum. 'I've got to go with Jonty.'

'Dunno wot we'll do,' Mr Wells grunted. 'They'll all rot on the bines.'

'Sorry,' said Mum. 'I don't *want* to go, I can tell you. I *like* hop-picking — and need the money.'

But Mr Wells had hobbled away, concerned only about the hops. Even the thought of an invasion did not seem more important.

'Get the truck, Bill,' said Mum, as she tucked the tokens and tally stick into her apron pocket. 'Pile the baskets and the stools in.'

'All the stools won't go,' protested Bill.

'O.K. — pile in what you can,' relented Mum. 'We'll have to carry the rest.'

'Don't usually carry all this in one go,' moaned Bill. 'We have two trips.'

'I know,' agreed Mum, 'but we haven't got *time* for two trips. We've *got* to get it all home in one.'

As she spoke, she was pushing the bines back and piling all of their stuff together.

'What a lot,' thought Emma. 'All this — and tomorrow too!'

Fran and Jonty rushed up the alley towards them.

'Dad's here. Dad's here,' they shouted.

'Thank goodness,' said Mum and her frown disappeared.

'*And* Mr Turner,' they added, as Babs and Fran shouted 'Dad's here,' in the next alley.

Dad appeared with his bike, still in his working overalls and dirty shoes.

'Just heard,' he said. 'Thought I'd better come and help.'

'Did the boss let you?' Mum asked anxiously.

'Well, he's got kids,' replied Dad, 'so he wanted to go off too. Sent us all home.'

'Nice of him,' said Mum. 'You know we've got to leave tomorrow? *Tomorrow*.' She was nearly in tears. Emma knew how she felt.

'I know, duck,' Dad said to her. 'Cheer up. P'raps it won't be for long.'

'But what will happen to you whilst we're away?' Mum went on anxiously.

'I'll live on spuds!' laughed Dad. 'I can cook those.'

'Yes, that's about all,' smiled Mum.

'Come on,' Dad said, piling things onto the truck. 'I'll tie this behind my bike. Bill, fix a couple of stools over your saddle and Emma take these two fold-up ones.'

'Fran,' called Mum, 'come up and get hold of this bag. It's not too heavy for you and Jonty, you can carry the sacks.'

27

Soon, all of their hop-picking goods were gathered up and they were ready for the trek home across the fields and through the orchards.

'Strange to be running away like this in the middle of hop-picking,' thought Emma. 'The last day is usually such fun, with bonfires, singing and rides in the farm cart.'

She had missed it once before when she had been suddenly whipped into hospital. She closed her mind to *that* nasty experience and hoped the evacuation would be happier.

She peered through the hop-poles to the Turners. They were still piling their things together. Mr Turner looked very black. He had come straight from the mine and had not been home to wash first. Emma could hardly recognise him, with his two white eyes peering out of his black face. But — he sounded the same when he called out, ' 'Bye you Barts, see you at eight o'clock tomorrow — and don't forget your gas masks.'

'Toodle-oo,' called Dad and they bumped and stumbled across the rough tracks of the hop-fields to join all of the other pickers hurriedly going home.

Chapter Three

LAST NIGHT AT HOME

FINALLY, they reached the passage by their house and gratefully, Emma dumped the stools in the shed. She left Dad and Bill to sort out the rest of the stuff and went into the kitchen to help Mum.

'Put the kettle on Emma,' said Mum. 'We'll be able to think better when we've had a cup of tea.'

'Before I scrub my hands?' Emma was surprised, because they usually had to clean their hands before they touched *anything* in the kitchen.

'Yes — let it boil whilst we scrub up,' said Mum, reaching for the Vim and soap.

They scrubbed away until the revolting black stains began to disappear from their palms and fingers.

'My nails are still black,' said Emma.

'I know,' said Mum. 'Have another go later.'

'My arms are all scratched and they sting when the soap gets into them,' went on Emma.

'Always the same,' sighed Mum. 'Hop bines *do* scratch.'

'What are we going to do about clothes?' asked Emma.

'That's what's been worrying me,' said Mum. 'You all

need new shoes and I was going to get them with the hoppin' money.'

'Good job my grant came through early and we got my Blankton uniform,' said Emma.

'Yes — you're all right,' said Mum, as she dried her hands, 'except for a coat, and you haven't got enough coupons for a coat — let alone the money.'

'I'd forgotten that,' said Emma, looking worried. 'My old one's brown — can't wear *that* over a navy blue school uniform.'

Mum was thinking hard. 'Bill's got a navy raincoat,' she said slowly. 'And Aunty Dot gave him another one that Harry had grown out of.'

'Mu–um — I can't wear a *boy's* raincoat,' Emma protested.

'Well,' said Mum. 'It's either that, or your old brown coat.'

Emma wanted to cry; she knew she would be *so* embarrassed *whichever* coat she took. But what was the good? Mum could not do anything else to help.

'O.K.,' she said reluctantly. 'I'll take Bill's.'

'You'll take my what?' Bill wanted to know as he came in the back door.

'Your navy raincoat,' replied Mum.

'But what about me?' Bill protested.

'You'll have to wear that old one of Harry's,' said Mum firmly.

'Oh — all right then,' said Bill, sounding disgruntled, but knowing he had no choice. When Mum sounded like that, her mind was made up.

The kettle whistled. Mum warmed the teapot and made the tea, then sat down with a piece of paper and a pencil.

'Let it stand,' she said 'and I'll make out a list of all the things we need to take.'

'Sure to forget *something*,' said Bill.

'What are we doing? Where are we going?' asked Jonty.

'You're going on a train in the morning,' said Emma.

'A train — goody good,' shouted Jonty.

'Where to?' asked Fran.

'We don't know,' replied Bill.

'But we *must* know,' said Fran. 'We can't buy tickets if we don't know where we're going,' she added, quite logically.

'And you can't go on a train without tickets,' said Jonty, a tone of finality to his voice.

'Well, this time,' said Dad coming into the living room, 'you don't need tickets and where you're going is a mystery.'

'I *love* mysteries,' said Fran.

'Not this sort,' muttered Bill.

'Fetch the mugs, Emma,' said Dad, 'and Bill you get the milk.'

'Jug, or condensed?' asked Bill, as he went into the kitchen.

'Let's make this special,' said Mum. 'Bring fresh.'

They sat round the table with their mugs of tea and ginger biscuits, whilst Mum finished her lists. She tore her paper into five pieces, gave them one each and kept one for herself.

'I can't read mine,' wailed Jonty.

'I know you can't,' said Mum. 'You just hold it and Emma will help you get the things.'

'Not much on my list,' said Bill.

'I know,' said Mum, 'but you've only *got* one pair of school trousers and blazer, so you can't take much more.'

31

For the next hour, they were all bustling around, collecting clothes and putting them in piles on their beds.

'What about bags?' asked Dad.

'Well, Jonty and I can share a case, Bill's got his haversack and Fran can have Aunt Bertha's leather bag,' replied Mum.

'That leaves Emma,' said Dad. 'She really needs a case for that school uniform.'

'Do you think Fanny Farmer would lend us one?' asked Mum, with a sudden inspiration.

'Well,' said Dad. '*I'm* not going to ask her! I've got to live next door to her when you've all gone. *Every* day she'll moan about the case that the Barts have pinched!'

'O.K.' said Mum. 'You're right. Not worth it.'

There was a knock at the front door.

'I'll go,' said Dad.

They listened and heard Mr King's voice. He was the school attendance officer and all of the children in the city were rather afraid of him.

'Wonder what *he* wants?' said Bill.

'What have you been up to?' asked Mum.

'Nothing,' Bill protested. 'Really — nothing.'

Mum looked doubtful. They heard the front door close and Dad re-appeared with a small case.

'Mr King thought we might need an extra suitcase,' he said. 'They haven't got to go away.'

'No children,' said Mum. 'Isn't that kind of him?'

'S'pose he's all right really,' admitted Bill.

'It's only his *job* that makes us all afraid of him,' said Emma.

She and Mum carefully packed her clothes into the case. All of the luggage was lined up in the hall, coats on top and gas-masks piled alongside.

'That's that much done,' said Mum. 'Now food.' As she went into the kitchen, the siren wailed out.

'Down the cellar,' said Dad. He opened the door and turned on the light.

'Oh Dad,' protested Bill, 'can't we go outside and watch?'

'*Please* Dad,' joined in Emma.

'It'll be all over when we come back,' said Bill. 'We'll have missed all the fun.'

'Look,' said Dad, relenting. 'I'll go out and see what's happening. If I think it's safe, I'll call you.' He took his hat from its peg on the cellar wall and went out of the back door.

'Do you think we can stay here for a bit?' called Mum. 'There's so much to do.'

'O.K.,' Dad shouted back. 'Just for now.'

'I *hate* it in that dirty, dark cellar with all the coal,' said Emma.

'I'm frightened down there,' cried Jonty.

'Funny that,' said Emma. 'I'm more frightened in the cellar than I am in the hop-garden, when I can *see* the planes fighting.'

'It's fun,' said Bill again.

'Not much fun for the pilots up there,' Mum reminded him.

'Yep,' he agreed. 'You sort of forget there are *men* in those planes.'

'And bombs,' said Emma. 'Jolly good job they don't want to drop them on us. We're not important enough here.'

'P'raps they think we might be, one day,' said Mum, as she began cutting slices of bread. 'That's why they're sending us away — just like they did the London children.'

'That reminds me,' said Bill, fishing in his trouser pocket. 'We didn't get any pieces of plane today, but we *did* get this.' He pulled out a piece of white, silky material.

'What on earth's that?' asked Emma.

'Piece of a parachute,' said Bill. 'It ripped on some trees as it came down and we climbed up to get some bits before the police sent us away.'

'Is it silk?' asked Mum, feeling it.

'Well,' said Bill. 'One of the policemen called it nylon.'

'What's nylon?' asked Emma.

'Dunno,' said Bill. 'Something new, I guess.'

Emma felt the small piece.

'Pity you didn't get a *big* piece,' she laughed. 'Could have made a petticoat out of it.'

Dad came in again.

'O.K.,' he said. 'The planes are pretty high up. You can come out, *but*, if I say IN — it's straight inside and down that cellar. No arguing.'

'And us,' begged Fran and Jonty.

'Just for a minute,' said Dad. 'Then you must come in to help Mum.'

'Coo — look at that,' cried Bill, as a small plane dived down towards an enemy plane, splattering bullets as it came and leaving a thin white trail behind it.

'He's got it,' yelled Bill, jumping up and down as the larger plane fell out of the V formation and hurtled towards the ground.

'Where's it coming down?' said Emma.

'Over there in Dockering Woods, I think,' said Dad, pointing across the allotments. 'Looks as if it'll hit those trees.'

The distant plane whined to the earth and there was a terrible explosion.

'Can I go, Dad?' asked Bill.

'Sorry boy,' said Dad. 'Not today.'

'Oh, Dad,' pleaded Bill. 'My last chance.'

'NOT-TO-DAY,' said Dad *very* firmly.

The planes were droning out of sight. The enemy V had gaps.

'Think three have been shot down,' said Bill.

'They may hit some more before they get to London,' said Emma, hopefully.

'Look at those Spitfires,' said Bill. 'I'd like to be a fighter pilot one day.' He gazed admiringly at the sky, as the small planes continued to spit bullets.

Soon, they could neither be seen, nor heard. The sound of the All Clear told them that there were no more enemy planes coming across the coast towards them.

Back in the kitchen, Mum was piling sandwiches onto greaseproof paper and sausage meat was splattering in the pan.

'Nearly ready,' she said. 'Lay the table Emma.'

At last they were all sitting round the table in the living room, tucking in to jacket potatoes with dripping and crispy pats of sausage meat.

Dad looked round at them all with a sad look on his face.

'Wonder where you'll all be tomorrow night,' he said. 'I'll miss you.'

'That's what I don't like,' said Mum. 'We'll all be separated.'

'And no-one will know where anyone else is,' said Bill, dolefully.

''cept Dad,' put in Emma. 'We'll all know that Dad is here.'

'Write to me as soon as you've got an address,' Dad said. 'Then I'll write to all of you.'

'It'll take ages,' said Mum. 'At least two weeks.'

'A lot can happen in two weeks, especially when there's a war on,' said Dad, the sad look returning to his face.

'Wish we, or somebody near us had a phone,' said Bill.

'Wouldn't it be easy — save all those letters.'

'Well we haven't,' said Dad, 'and not likely to have.'

'Only important people have phones,' said Emma. 'It's like cars and bathrooms.'

'Perhaps one day,' laughed Mum, 'you'll all be important people.'

She collected the plates and brought in jelly and custard for pudding. As she put it down on the table, Dad said, 'What about ration books?'

Mum nearly dropped the jelly. 'Heavens no,' she gasped. 'I knew we'd forget something important. Emma, fetch the dishes whilst I get them out.'

Mum fished in her shopping bag and brought out their

ration books. She gave Dad his and went into the hall to put the others on top of the cases.

'I'll put them inside later,' she said, as she began dishing out the pudding. 'Would have been terrible to go without them.'

Washing-up, bedtime stories and bed, happened fairly quickly after supper.

'We'll all need to be up early in the morning,' said Mum, as she came to kiss them goodnight.

'It's a long walk to the West Station,' said Dad, as he joined her.

'And we've got all those bags to carry,' murmered Emma sleepily.

Chapter Four

DAD — LEFT ALONE

'WAKE up.' Mum was gently shaking Emma. 'Come on you two,' she said, as she tried to rouse the sleeping Fran.

Emma rubbed her eyes. 'What's the time?' she asked.

'Half past six,' replied Mum. 'I've brought up some hot water, so if you two wash here, the men can use the kitchen.'

'So Bill and Jonty are men now are they!,' laughed Emma, as she climbed out of bed, lifted the cold water jug onto the floor and began to pour the hot water into the basin.

Mum smiled as she went out of the bedroom door.

'Good job they're not all shaving yet,' she said. 'Dad takes long enough!'

Quickly Emma washed and dressed. She emptied the water from the basin into the bucket and poured more hot water out for Fran.

'Come on, lazy bones,' she said. 'Out you get. No time to turn over today. Long way to go.'

She pulled back the bedclothes, took Fran's legs and dragged her out of bed.

'You get washed. I'll make the bed,' she said.

'Thought it had to air,' said Fran sleepily.

'Not today. No time,' said Emma. 'Wonder when we'll sleep in it again?'

Fran was standing at the basin ready to wash her face.

'Where will we sleep tonight, Em?' she asked tearfully.

'Don't know, Fran,' said Emma. 'Cheer up. It *might* be somewhere nice — and at least we'll be together.'

Fran gave a weak smile and began to rub her face with a flannel. Emma finished the bed and looked at herself in the mirror. She looked quite smart in her new Blankton school uniform. She thought, 'Didn't think I'd be wearing it for the first time on the day I was going away. Just — going away.'

It was a very nasty feeling, like playing Blind Man's Buff. When they twisted you round, you had no idea which direction you were walking in and who you were going to touch. But that was a game — and fun. *This* was not.

Emma went downstairs and found Bill and Jonty already washed and dressed.

'Boiled eggs this morning,' announced Jonty. 'Goody.'

'Where did Mum get fresh eggs from?' asked the surprised Emma.

'Well, Dad saw Mr Winter last night, after we were all in bed and *he* gave them to *us*, as a special going-away treat,' replied Bill.

'Nice of him,' said Emma.

'Probably glad to see the back of us,' laughed Bill.

'He'll miss us when all his chickens get out,' retorted Emma. 'No one to catch them.'

'*You* don't actually *catch* many,' Bill reminded her.

'No,' returned Emma, 'but I flap my pinny* so that they run into *your* hands!'

---

*pinafore or apron

'Now stop it, you two,' said Mum, as she brought in the toast and eggs. 'Where's Fran?'

'Nearly ready,' said Emma. They heard her bump slowly down the stairs.

Dad finished his shaving and sat down for breakfast. They were all rather quiet, partly because they were eating quickly and partly because they were not sure what to say. It was the strangest family breakfast they had ever had.

'We're all afraid,' thought Emma. 'We just don't know what's going to happen.'

Mum looked at the clock. 'Seven o'clock,' she said. 'We must leave here at quarter past, so as soon as you've finished, take your things into the kitchen and wash your hands.'

There was a quarter of an hour of bustling. Finally, they stood in the hall, gas masks round their shoulders. Dad gave them all a hug and a kiss.

'May not be able to do that at the station,' he said gently. 'Lots of people around. Take care all of you.' He quickly turned and went out through the back door to collect his bike from the shed.

They were all very near to tears. Mum blew her nose, Emma rubbed her hands across her eyes and Bill blinked hard, *very* hard.

'Pick up your bags,' said Mum in a low voice and opened the front door. She banged it shut behind them and none of them knew when they would go back through it. They stood and waited for Dad to come up the passage by the side of the house.

It was a long walk to the West Station and, with every step, Emma knew she was walking away from home. Her legs moved reluctantly, they did *not* want to go past the Norman castle, down Castle Street, into Beer Cart Lane, towards the High Street. As they all turned to go through the Westgate Towers, Emma's legs nearly stopped. Once through those towers, they were only a few minutes away from the station — and that train.

The Barts were surrounded by lots of other families, with bags and cases in their hands and gas-masks bumping up and down on their backs. There was none of the usual cheery chatting and laughter, just a glum silence and the odd wave to friends.

Finally, they reached Station Road and saw queues and queues of women and children. Men were standing around, or going from group to group, having a quiet word with different members of the family.

'How do we know which queue to join?' asked Emma.

'I think they've all got notices by them,' replied Dad.

As they got nearer they sould see

— **BLANKTON BOYS**

— **BLANKTON GIRLS**

— **Mothers and young children**

41

Dad stood his bike on the edge of the pavement and said, 'This is it.'

He gave Mum and Jonty a big hug, then Emma, Fran and Bill. Mum was crying as she kissed the girls and Bill goodbye.

'We'll see you — somewhere,' she said. 'We'll all write to Dad — and then we'll see . . .' Her voice trailed off.

'We have no idea,' thought Emma, 'no idea at all, whether we'll be near, or miles and miles away from each other.'

'Your queue girls,' said Dad and he guided them to the back. Emma and Fran waved to the others and watched, as first Bill, then Mum and Jonty, joined other queues.

Dad stood talking to Mum for a few minutes, then went across to an ARP* Warden, who looked official. The Warden kept shaking his head and shrugging his shoulders to Dad's questions.

'He doesn't look any happier,' thought Emma, as he returned to Mum and Jonty. She watched their faces as they spoke to each other. Emma had seldom seen either of them look so unhappy.

Dad moved across to Bill's queue and finally, came to the girls.

'Thought I might find out a bit more,' he said, 'but the Warden doesn't know any more than we do. All he knows is that he's got to help get you all on the trains. Where those trains are going to, he has no idea.'

'How long?' asked Emma tearfully. Time really *was* running out.

'About five minutes,' replied Dad. 'I'll wave — that's all I can do.'

Dad did not usually seem helpless. Whatever happened you knew *he* would find a way to solve the problem.

*Air Raid Precautions

'Not today,' thought Emma. 'Other people are in charge. Telling us what to do.'

A whistle blew and a tall man in uniform, stood on a little platform with a loud speaker. He announced , 'Those not travelling, please move away from the queues and stand on the pavement.'

Reluctantly, Dad gave the girls a last hug, blew kisses to Mum and Jonty and touched Bill's shoulder on his way to the pavement. He stood there, holding his bike. There were lots of men around him, but they all seemed so lonely.

The tall man in uniform lifted his loud speaker to his mouth again.

'Blankton Boys — ready,' he announced.

The boys and teachers picked up bags and cases and filed across to the station entrance. Dad slowly waved to Bill as he followed the others through the large door towards the waiting trains.

'Mothers and young children,' said the tall man.

With feelings of panic inside her, Emma grabbed Fran's hand as she watched Mum and Jonty walking through those big doors, waving to Dad.

'Nearly us,' thought Emma. 'Nearly us, then poor Dad will get on his bike and ride away.'

'When's our turn?' whispered Fran.

'Soon,' Emma whispered back. 'Very soon.'

'BLANKTON GIRLS,' announced the man in uniform.

Emma and Fran picked up their bags and followed the others. As they waved to Dad, Emma could feel the tears running down her cheeks — and Dad's lips were trembling.

'Three times he's waved to the queues,' she thought as they followed the others through the big doors. She wanted to turn round for one last wave, but it was no good. Girls, girls and more girls were coming through behind them.

That was it. Emma could imagine Dad, getting on his bike and riding off down Station Road — alone.

Chapter Five

TRAIN JOURNEY INTO THE UNKNOWN

THE queue suddenly stopped and they heard a train whistle, then 'puff' and 'puff', before it steamed off. The line of girls moved slowly forward and stopped again, as another train puffed, puffed and whistled. It pulled out of the station and the Blankton Girls moved forward onto the empty platform. A third train steamed in.

'The others have gone,' thought Emma. 'I wonder where to?'

'Stand back. Stand back,' shouted the porter and Emma tried to do as she was told, but only managed to stand on the toes of the girl behind.

'Ouch,' said the the girl and Emma turned round.

'Sorry,' she said.

The girl behind said, 'I should *think so*,' in a very posh voice. Emma blushed and felt worse than ever.

'I hope,' she thought desperately, and held Fran's hand tightly, 'they're not *all* going to be horrid.'

The train squeaked to a stop and the porter said, 'Right, girls, In you get.'

With their bags, gas-masks and coats, they stumbled into the corridors. The haughty sounding girl pushed in front of Fran and Emma and sat down in the nearest compartment.

'Come on, Fran,' whispered Emma. 'Not there,' and moved on to the next compartment. It was almost full — just two seats left. Emma and Fran sat down with their bags on their knees.

'Let me take those,' said a friendly voice. Emma looked up and saw a ginger-haired girl smiling down at her.

'Hello, Mary,' she said and felt so relieved. At least they were going on this horrid journey with someone nice!

Mary took Emma's case, coat and gas-mask and put them up on the luggage rack. She piled Fran's things on top.

'There you are,' she said. 'Now you'll be much more comfortable.'

'Girls,' she went on, looking round the compartment, 'this is Emma — and her sister Fran. I'm Mary.'

The girls looked across with friendly eyes and went round introducing themselves.

'Peggy'

'Brenda'

'Eileen'

'Sylvia'

'Audrey'

Emma hoped she would not get them muddled.

'I'm new,' she said shyly. 'I don't really know anyone.'

'I'm new too,' said Peggy. 'But I'm lucky, Eileen's my big sister.'

'And I'm Mary's friend,' laughed Eileen.

'There you are,' Mary said. 'You know us already.'

The train whistled and jolted forward and Mary plonked back onto the seat, nearly sitting on Eileen's lap.

'Careful. Don't squash me,' Eileen teased. They all laughed, which was just as well, because the train was slowly pulling out of the station and Emma was sure that *none* of them really felt like laughing.

She looked out of the window and watched as they slowly passed the narrow houses in Station Road and then pulled towards the level crossing. She looked at the people standing waiting whilst the train crossed — and suddenly shot up.

'Dad,' she shouted and pushed her hand out of the tiny open window, waving frantically.

'Dad,' she called — and he saw her. His face broke into a smile and he waved and waved until the train had steamed out of sight.

'You lucky thing,' said Eileen.

'Fancy your Dad being there,' said Peggy.

'Bet he was pleased,' grinned Mary.

'So was I,' said Emma — and smiled, feeling *much* happier.

Their heads were all turned towards the window. They watched the tall tower of the cathedral gradually get smaller and smaller, as they steamed away towards — where?

'Wonder when we'll see that again,' murmured Mary.

'Wonder where we're going,' said Eileen thoughtfully.

'Will it be the same place as the boys?' joined in Audrey. 'My brother's with them.'

'And ours,' said Emma.

'How old is he?' asked Audrey.

'Nearly thirteen,' replied Emma.

'Same age as mine — and me,' said Audrey. 'We're twins. What's your brother's name?'

'Bill Barton,' said Emma.

Audrey laughed. 'I've heard about him,' she said, '*and* Jimmy Turner. They get up to all sorts of pranks.'

'S'pose they do,' agreed Emma. 'Don't think we hear about all of them.'

'My Mum's gone on one of the trains with my little brother and sister,' said Brenda.

'And ours,' said Emma, 'with our little brother.'

'Seems awful, doesn't it,' said Mary. 'All on different trains.'

'And not knowing whether we're all going to end up at the same place,' said Brenda, sadly.

'When Dad went into the Army,' said Peggy, 'he went off and we were all left at home together.'

'Now,' said Emma, 'it's us going off and our Dad's left at home alone.'

'Funny old war,' said Mary.

'Don't like it,' said Eileen. 'Not one little bit.'

The door of the compartment was suddenly pulled back.

'Good morning, girls,' said the haughty voice of Miss Pring. 'I'm the teacher in charge of this section of the train and will be coming along at regular intervals.'

'Good morning, Miss Pring.'

'Thank you, Miss Pring.'

'Yes, Miss Pring,' said the girls.

Miss Pring looked round the compartment and her eyes fell on Emma.

'Oh,' she said, with a slight twist to her lips, 'you *do* look clean today.' She closed the door and went away.

Emma felt her face burning and tears filling her eyes.

'The beast,' said Mary viciously.

'She's a nasty, nasty woman,' agreed Eileen. 'Ignore her Emma, if you can. We all know what she's like.'

Emma tried to smile. 'Thanks,' she said. 'Thanks.'

Fran looked around, not really sure what was happening.

'It's all right, Fran,' said Mary gently. 'Don't worry. Some teachers are nice people — others are horrid. She's one of the horrid ones.'

'I don't know why people like her ever *become* teachers,' said Eileen.

Suddenly, the train jolted to a halt. It stood — and stood — and stood. Then, it reversed back into a railway siding, in fits and starts. The brakes squealed on and the engine let out a huge puff of smoke that blew back past the windows. As the smoke cleared away, they could hear the sound of another train on the main line.

They stood up and looked out. An engine was pulling dozens of wagons. On each wagon was a huge khaki tank, covered with camouflage. Green and brown paint was streaked across and netting, with little green artificial leaves, was draped over each tank.

' 'spect they're going down to the coast,' said Mary.

'They're getting us out and moving the tanks in,' said Eileen.

They watched the tanks chug by and then, with a whistle, their train lurched forward, back on to the main line. Relieved to be on their way, the girls watched the scenery change from the fields, orchards and hop-fields, to houses, houses and more houses of a big city.

'This must be London,' said Emma.

'Yes, it is,' said Mary. 'I've been here once.'

'I haven't.' 'Nor me,' said some of the others.

They looked out to see famous buildings that they might recognise, but sadly, the nearer they got to the middle of London, the more they saw bombed buildings and ruins.

'Glad that hasn't happened to us,' said Audrey.

'Hope it doesn't happen whilst we're away,' said Emma. 'People get hurt.' She was thinking of Dad.

The girls kept looking at the bombed buildings, until the train entered a long, dark tunnel.

Mary jumped up and shut the window.

'Don't want all those blacks from the smoke in here,' she said.

As the train chugged out of the tunnel with a whistle, they could hear the sound of the siren, wailing up and down.

'Hope they don't drop any bombs whilst we're in London,' said Brenda.

'Will the train stop?' Mary wondered.

'Dunno,' said Eileen. 'P'raps if the planes are overhead.'

The train kept going and they heard the distant sound of gunfire. Instead of it becoming louder, it became fainter, as they reached the open countryside again.

'Should think we got through London just in time,' remarked Sylvia.

Eileen nodded and then said, 'Now, are we going north, south, or west?'

Emma thought, 'She's clever. Trying to make us think of other things.'

'If we know that,' Eileen went on, 'we'll have a guessing game about where we're going.'

'I know,' said Mary, jumping up. 'My pocket compass is in my haversack.'

'Fancy thinking of that, with everything else,' Sylvia marvelled.

'Well, I didn't actually *think* of it,' said Mary, pulling down her haversack from the rack. 'It was in here, from the last time I went to Guide camp. Thought I might as well leave it there.'

'We might be able to go to Guides — wherever we're going,' said Eileen.

Mary pulled out her pocket compass.

'Right,' she said. 'Let's see.'

They all stood up and crowded round.

The arrow pointed west.

Chapter Six

SLOUGH – BRISTOL – OR WALES?

THE train suddenly screeched to a halt again.

'More tanks,' said Eileen.

They waited — and waited — and waited. The train did *not* reverse into a siding. No trains passed on the other track. The fields to the left and right looked empty, with just a few buildings on the horizon. Mary looked at her watch.

'We've been here for over half an hour,' she said.

'I'm hungry,' said Audrey.

'Let's eat our sandwiches,' said Eileen. 'Help to pass the time.'

They rummaged around and brought out packages of various sizes. Emma unwrapped theirs and offered one to Fran, who peeped inside to see what was in the middle.

'Marmite,' she said.

'Peanut butter in some,' said Emma. As they munched, she looked out of the window and saw four jeeps bouncing across the field towards the railway line.

'Look,' she said, pointing, 'What's happening?'

Mary stood up and peered out of the window.

'They're going alongside the track, way up in front of the train,' she reported.

Eileen stood beside her and peered into the distance.

'Can you see a wrecked plane in that field over there?' she asked.

Mary followed her pointing finger. 'Yes,' she said 'I can just see the tail pointing up. The cockpit must be buried in the ground.'

The compartment door opened and Miss Pring appeared.

'The delay is caused by an unexploded bomb near the line,' she announced.. 'The Army has sent in troops to deal with it, but I am not sure how long we will have to wait. Just be patient.'

'Yes, Miss Pring.'

'Thank you Miss Pring,' said the girls as the door closed.

'If that had been Miss Plath,' grumbled Audrey, 'we could have talked to her about that plane over there.'

'Not Pringle,' agreed Mary. 'Can't talk to her about *anything.*'

'It's just — Yes Miss Pring — No Miss Pring — Three bags full, Miss Pring,' said Eileen and everyone laughed.

The door opened again. It was the posh girl from the next compartment.

'You have no right to speak about Miss Pring like that,' she said in a stuck-up voice. 'I Shall report you.'

'Now listen, Virginia,' said Mary firmly. 'You might be Pringle's pet — we don't mind that. But, today, there are more important things to think about than you being spiteful and Pringle being so toffee-nosed that we can't talk to her.'

Virginia slammed the door shut without another word. Emma gazed admiringly at Mary. Fancy having the courage to say that to a girl like Virginia!

'That's the end of her. I hope,' said Mary. 'Now let's

think about something really interesting.'

She stood up again and looked out of the window.

'Can't see,' she said and stood on the seat. She opened the little top window and poked her ginger head outside.

'The jeeps are way up the track,' she reported. 'I can see them round the bend. The soldiers are out, kneeling down and doing things.'

She jumped back down.

'At least we know,' said Eileen.

'Wonder how long it'll take us to get where we're going?' said Audrey as they carried on munching.

'That's it,' said Eileen. 'Where are we going?'

'West,' replied Mary.

'What places are west of London?' asked Sylvia.

'Wales,' said Audrey. 'My grandma lives there.'

'Well, if we're going as far as Wales,' said Mary, 'and stopping as many times as this, we won't get there 'til tomorrow!'

'What about Bristol?' asked Peggy.

'Yep,' said Eileen. 'That's west and a bit nearer.'

'Or Gloucester?' put in Sylvia.

'Yes — west — and even nearer,' agreed Mary.

Emma did not say anything. She really did not know which places were north, south, or west of London. What a lot she had to learn!

'Slough,' added Audrey. 'Must be nearly there now. My uncle and aunt live in Slough and we sometimes go in to see them on our way down to Wales.'

'Do you have a car then?' asked Eileen in surprise.

'Just a little one,' said Audrey. 'It's a tight fit for all of us — and it doesn't like going up hills. But Dad needs one for his work. He's a doctor.'

'Right then,' said Eileen. 'You can think of the other places you go through on your way down to Wales.'

Audrey thought hard and said, 'London, Slough, Reading —.'

'We haven't mentioned Reading before.' Mary interrupted her. 'Go on.'

'Swindon, Cheltenham, Gloucester — then Wales,' she finished. 'Think that's all the big places.'

'O.K.,' said Eileen, taking a notebook and pencil out of her pocket.

'Now, I want you all to tell me which place you think we're going to. When we get off the train, we'll see who's right.'

Emma began to think of the places mentioned and whispered to Fran, who was not quite sure about the game, 'We'll say the same place.'

The others began to make decisions.

'Wales,' said Audrey. 'I'll see my grandma.'

'Slough,' said Sylvia, 'because Audrey said we're nearly there.'

The others laughed.

'Then I'll go for Reading,' said Mary. 'That's the place you gave after Slough, wasn't it Audrey?'

'I *think* that's right,' said Audrey.

'Now, Peggy,' said Eileen. 'Where are you going?'

'I don't know,' said Peggy. 'I don't want to go to any of them very much.'

'Let's say Bristol, then,' said Eileen. 'You and me. We'd better stick together.'

'Now, Emma,' said Mary. 'What about you and Fran?'

Emma suddenly remembered. 'Gloucester,' she exclaimed. 'My uncle lives there. He did write to Mum and Dad soon after the war started, saying we could go and live with him if we needed to be evacuated.'

'Why didn't you go then?' asked Sylvia.

'Well, we didn't need to go then,' replied Emma.

'Evacuees were coming to us. Then now — there wasn't time to do anything.'

'Except just do as you were told,' agreed Eileen.

'Brenda — your turn,' said Mary.

'Any places left?' asked Brenda.

'Yes,' said Eileen, looking at her notebook, 'Swindon, or Cheltenham.'

'Dunno,' said Brenda.

'Well, Swindon's nearer and Cheltenham's nicer,' said Audrey.

'Right — Swindon,' said Brenda. 'Nearer now — and nearer to go home one day.'

Carefully, Eileen put her notebook back in her pocket, then laughed.

'When the train starts, we'd better see if we're *still* going west,' she said. 'They *might* change their minds.'

Mary stood on the seat and put her head through the window.

'They're piling things into their jeeps,' she announced. 'The first jeep's off.'

Sure enough, they saw the jeep bouncing back across the field towards the crashed plane.

'The others are coming,' called Mary.

'Must have finished,' said Emma, as Mary climbed down.

They all watched, as the jeeps headed back to the plane. The guard blew his whistle. Steam belched out of the engine, back along the train and in through their open window.

'Quick, shut it,' said Eileen and Mary slammed it, speckles of black on her cheeks.

'Ouch,' she said. 'A piece of black has gone in my eye.'

'Sit down,' said Eileen, pulling the handkerchief out of her pocket and twisting one corner. She held Mary's eye wide open and poked the corner in.

'Got it,' she said and triumphantly, displayed the little black speck.

'Still hurts,' said Mary and her eye was watering.

''spect it does,' said Eileen, 'but at least the dirt's out.'

'Clever thing,' said Sylvia.

'Oh well,' said Eileen. 'Haven't got my First Aid badge for nothing.'

The train was now jolting forward and was soon back to its normal rhythm — br – d – d – d

br – d – d – d

br – d – d – d

They passed through a station.

'Where was that?' asked Audrey.

'Dunno,' said Mary. 'All the signs and notices have been taken down.'

'Makes it difficult,' said Eileen. 'We can only guess.'

'Let's guess Slough,' said Sylvia. 'That means I'm wrong.'

'Look at my compass,' said Mary, passing it across to Eileen with one hand and keeping the other over her weeping eye.

Eileen looked. 'Still going west,' she said.

'Reading, next,' said Audrey.

'Hope it's Reading,' yawned Eileen. 'Feels as if we've been going for *hours*.'

'I'll be falling asleep before we arrive,' said Mary.

'Was a jolly early start,' said Sylvia.

The compartment door was pulled open again.

'Clean up that mess, girls,' said Miss Pring. 'You *must* have finished your sandwiches by now.'

'Yes, Miss Pring.'

'Certainly, Miss Pring.'

'Of course, Miss Pring,' they said.

'Mary, collect the rubbish and make sure you take it off the train with you,' continued Miss Pring.

Mary took her hand off her weeping eye.

'What's the matter with you, girl?' said Miss Pring, spotting it. 'Not a cry-baby. I hope. You are too old for that.'

'Mary had a piece of grit in her eye,' explained Eileen.

'She should *not* have been leaning out of the window then,' returned Miss Pring and slammed the compartment door shut.

'Beast,' burst out Eileen.

'Don't let Virginia hear you,' laughed Mary. 'She'll "report you" ' she mimicked.

Emma was amazed to see how these two big girls coped with nasty people like Miss Pring and Virginia.

'Hope I'm like that when I'm their age,' she thought.

Chapter Seven

MYSTERY SOLVED — BISCUITS THE CLUE

IT seemed a long time before the train began to slow down again. The girls had stopped laughing and talking. Emma was finding it difficult to keep her eyes open and Fran had fallen asleep with her head on Emma's shoulder.

'Another big town,' said Mary.

'It's nearly six o'clock,' said Eileen. 'Hope this is where we're stopping. I'm fed up with this train.'

At the sound of their voices, Emma sat up and looked at the houses on each side of the track.

'Where are we?' she thought. 'Will it be here? Are Mum and the others here already — or have they gone somewhere else?'

The train's brakes squealed, as it began travelling even more slowly.

'Think this is Reading,' said Audrey. 'I *think* the train's stopping.'

The engine whistled and started puffing smoke again. They all looked out of the window and saw that they were pulling into a big station. The brakes screeched and the train stopped by the platform.

Miss Pring's voice was heard in the corridor.

'Remain seated,' she shouted. 'Remain seated until you are given further instructions.'

They heard a carriage door open and saw her striding along the platform. Mary stood up and peered out.

'Remain seated,' mimicked Eileen. 'Remain seated.'

They all laughed — and Mary continued to peep out.

'Pringle's talking to Duch,' she informed them. 'A man in uniform is going up to them. Miss Plath has joined them.'

'Go on. Go on,' said Audrey. 'You're doing a good job.'

'Where are we, do you think?' asked Sylvia.

'No idea,' replied Mary. 'All the station signs have been taken down.'

'What's happening?' asked Eileen.

'The man in the uniform is pointing,' said Mary. 'Pringle's coming back this way.' Quickly she pulled her head back and sat down with the others. Miss Pring walked past their compartment and glared in.

'Hope she didn't see me,' said Mary. 'That's the trouble with ginger hair. Too easily recognised.'

They heard Miss Pring's voice.

'Get your cases down,' she ordered. 'File out quickly and quietly onto the platform.'

The scramble began and soon they were all out of the train, being marshalled into crocodiles to file off the platform, through the lobby and onto the pavement outside. Emma took Fran's hand and tried to stay close to Mary and Eileen.

'Silence, girls,' called Miss Cannon. 'Coaches are coming to collect us and take us to a church hall, where we will be met by local officials. Stand still quietly until they arrive.'

'Wonder where we are?' Mary whispered to Eileen.

Audrey's voice came quietly over Emma's shoulder.

'Where?' Mary and Eileen shouted, forgetting Miss Cannon's orders. The girls usually called their headmistress Duch, short for The Duchess. Emma thought this probably started many years ago as a compliment, because Miss Cannon was certainly a dignified, stately lady.

'Silence, girls,' Miss Cannon said again.

'Reading,' Audrey whispered.

'How do you know?' Mary whispered back.

'See that big biscuit factory,' whispered Audrey. '*That* is in the middle of Reading.'

'Clever girl,' whispered Eileen.

'Quiet there,' bellowed Miss Pring.

Fortunately, the coaches began to arrive and one pulled up by the kerb, near to where Emma was standing.

'On you get,' said Miss Pring. 'Mary and Eileen first. The others follow on.'

Thankfully, Emma and Fran climbed the steps behind the two big girls and turned to see Audrey and Peggy close behind.

'Goody,' said Audrey. 'We're all together.'

Emma felt glad that she included her and Fran in this group of friends.

Soon the coach was full. Cases were piled on the racks. Gas-masks and coats were on their knees. Engines started and they all shook a bit with the vibration, but they were soon chugging off through the streets of Reading.

'It's good to put a name to the place,' thought Emma. 'Wonder if Mum and the others are here — or in Swindon, Bristol, or Gloucester. Funny if they landed up in Gloucester. What a surprise for Uncle Will!'

They bumped along and after a time, pulled round in front of a church. The coach stopped and the driver opened the door.

'Everyone out,' he said. 'Take your bags and gas-masks with you. Don't leave anything behind.'

'Crocodiles, girls,' ordered Miss Pring. Miss Cannon stood talking to an A.R.P. warden and then walked with him through the open doors of the church hall. They stood and waited.

Emma felt tired — very tired and she looked down at Fran's pale face.

'She must feel as if she's sleep walking.'

Fran was usually so lively and bubbly, but had hardly said a word all day. Emma knew that *she* had found it hard, but it must have been much worse for Fran — all of the big girls playing games that she did not understand —cracking jokes that did not make her laugh. Emma knew that, for as long as they were away, she must not just think about what was happening to herself but remember, that for Fran it was much worse.

'I've got to be like Mum, Dad, Jonty and Bill all rolled into one!' Emma sighed. She certainly had not thought of all that when she had suggested Fran coming with her.

Miss Pring's voice disturbed her thoughts.

'Forward girls,' she boomed out. Emma and Fran followed the crocodile forward into the gloomy church hall. They joined the other girls who were sitting cross-legged on the floor, taking care to sit near Mary, Eileen and Peggy.

When all of the girls were seated. Miss Cannon stood on the platform.

'Silence girls,' she said. 'Now that we have finally arrived in Reading ...' At this, there was a buzz around the room.

'Reading!'

'Reading!'

'Where's that?'

'Silence girls,' went on Miss Cannon. 'Yes — I said Reading, which is to the west of London. The people here are being very kind and have invited us to stay in their homes. I want you all to be good, considerate guests of their families.

'Remember — you *are* guests and I expect all Blankton girls to know how a guest should behave.

'Shortly, your hosts and hostesses will arrive to select the girls they would like to have in their homes.'

'Select!'

'Choose!'

'Like an auction!'

These whispers surrounded Emma and she felt desperately unhappy again. Suppose no-one chose her and Fran?

'We have been very fortunate,' went on Miss Cannon, 'in that the headmistress of Reading High School for Girls has invited us to share their premises. We may stay at the High School until we are allowed to return to East Kent.

'I am sure you will agree with me that this is a most generous gesture. I shall expect every Blankton girl to obey the rules of *both* schools, without question.'

Miss Plath stepped forward to speak to her and Miss Cannon nodded in reply, waving her arm to the kitchen door at the far end of the hall. Four ladies appeared with trolleys laden with tea-pots, cups and biscuits.

'Tea and biscuits will now be served,' announced Miss Cannon. 'Form an orderly queue and then return to your same positions on the floor.'

At last they were all seated again. 'I didn't realise how thirsty I was,' said Mary.

'Haven't had a proper drink since breakfast,' said Eileen 'and that seems a life-time away.'

'Quiet girls,' ordered Miss Cannon. 'One or two more points before your hosts and hostesses arrive.

'As you leave the hall, you will all be given a printed card. You must address this to your parents at home. On the other side, fill in the name and address of your host and hostess.'

At this point, a number of people began to file into the hall.

Miss Cannon went on, 'The post is taking a very long time at the moment, due to enemy action in London and the disruption of trains. You should, therefore, post your cards tomorrow. It will *still* take about *two weeks* for the cards to arrive. If your brothers, sisters and mothers have also been evacuated, it is going to take quite a long time before you discover where they are.'

Emma's heart sank. Two weeks before Dad knew where they all were — and even longer before *she* knew where Mum, Bill and Jonty were — even if they were all in the same town! Suppose there was an invasion and the cards never got to Dad? They might never see each other again. Her eyes filled with tears at the thought.

'One last point,' said Miss Cannon, as more people came in. 'When you take the card, also take the piece of paper with instructions about school tomorrow.

'I expect to see *every* girl at the High School tomorrow, by nine o'clock. We *might* have been evacuated, but school goes on.'

Miss Plath came forward and Miss Cannon sat down.

'Now girls,' she said. 'I am sure we are delighted to see the people of Reading who are going to welcome us into their homes.' She began to clap and all of the girls joined in.

'Just stay seated,' she said, 'and they will come round and choose girls who will fit into their family.'

She smiled. 'If it takes a long time for you to be chosen, don't worry. The right person *will* come — and I'm sure that you'll all be very happy.'

She went across to the crowd of people and had a few words. The girls sat looking nervously across the room.

'Why can't we choose them?' whispered Mary.

'Some look much nicer than others,' whispered Eileen back.

Emma held Fran's hand tightly. She knew that she was not going to like the next few minutes *at all*.

Chapter Eight

CHOSEN AT LAST

HUSBANDS and wives, wives on their own and elderly ladies, began moving around the hall amongst the girls. They bent down and talked to some, then went away and had little chats between themselves.

Gradually, girls began to stand up, take their coats, cases and gas-masks, and walk towards the door with their hosts and hostesses. Miss Plath sat there, behind a table, smiling and handing out cards, with slips of paper, as they left.

A jolly-looking lady came up to Mary. 'Hello,' she said. 'Are you on your own?'

'Well, yes,' said Mary. 'I don't *need* to be if you want two, or more of us.'

'Oh no,' laughed the lady. 'I've only space for one! But all of my children are red-heads, so you'd fit in very well. How about it?'

'Fine,' said Mary standing up. Emma had not seen her looking as unsure of herself before, almost as if she did *not* want to go off alone, but would rather be with a friend. She had no choice — and fortunately, the lady looked nice.

' 'Bye,' said Mary. 'See you all at school tomorrow.'

Emma watched her collect her card and go out of the

door. She felt lonelier than ever and gripped Fran's hand hard.

A man and lady were now talking to Eileen and Peggy. They looked a serious couple, as if there would not be much fun and laughing in their house.

'P'raps I'm wrong,' thought Emma. 'They might be just as worried as we are about all this.'

Eileen and Peggy were standing up. 'See you tomorrow,' they said and went off with a little wave, but no smiles.

'No-one wants us,' whispered Audrey, as the number of girls sitting on the floor dwindled. Then, an old lady came and took her hand.

'Come on, m'dear,' she said. 'I'll have you.' That was it — and Audrey walked with her towards the door.

'Oh dear,' thought Emma, feeling very upset. 'Do we look *so* awful?'

'Hi, don't look so sad,' said a cheery voice and Emma turned round to see a very pretty lady standing beside her.

'Is this your sister?' she asked.

'Yes,' replied Emma. 'This is Fran — she's eight. I'm Emma and I'm eleven.'

'I think you're just right for me,' said the lady, smiling and nodding, so that her pretty black curls bobbed up and down on her collar.

'You look tired,' she said to Fran. 'Missing Mum too, I expect.' She helped them both to their feet.

'You've got a bit stiff sitting down there. Now let me take your cases and we'll get home as quickly as we can.'

As they went with her to the door, Emma felt really relieved. They had found a nice lady who wanted them.

'We won't have to walk,' said the lady, 'because my friend is here with his car to take us home.'

'A ride in a car!' thought Emma. 'Weren't they lucky?'

They collected their cards from Miss Plath and went out.

A man was standing by a black car. He opened the door as they came towards him.

'Hello. I'm Charlie,' he said. 'Climb in.'

They climbed in the back, whilst their hostess and Charlie got into the front. Emma had only been in two cars in her life before — Aunty Tiny's and Mrs Bright's. Aunty Tiny was a midwife and had a tiny little car, so that she could get around quickly to houses in the country villages to see all those mothers and their new babies.

Mrs Bright was *very* rich and had a big car. Aunt Dolly was her maid. Emma knew that *she* did not want to be a maid when she grew up. She never wanted to wear a black dress, a little white apron and a little, lacy white cap whilst she served tea to stuck-up ladies, saying — 'Yes, Ma-am.' 'No-Ma-am.' 'Did you ring, Ma-am' — all the time.

Once, when Emma was visiting Aunty Dolly. Mrs Bright

had taken her for a ride in her car, with a nasty, posh boy. She loved the car, but *hated* the boy and wished she had not been chosen for that horrible treat.

Now as they bumped along, she felt strangely happy. It seemed as if things were not going to be too bad after all. Their hostess turned round and smiled.

'You O.K.?' she asked. They nodded and she went on. 'I'm Mrs Philips — but everyone calls me Phil, so you might as well do the same.'

'Thank you, Mrs Philips,' said Emma.

'Phil,' laughed Charlie.

'What time did you leave home?' asked Phil.

'We got on the train at eight o'clock, so it felt a jolly long way,' said Emma. 'And we'd walked to the station before.'

'Did your Mum and Dad take you to the train?' asked Phil. 'Yes,' Emma told her, 'then we all got on different trains and left Dad standing there alone,' she finished sadly.

'Poor Dad,' sympathised Phil. 'Let's hope he's got lots of friends.'

'She really does sound nice,' thought Emma.

'Nearly there,' said Charlie, as they went round another corner and pulled up at a house with a little front garden and white gate. The car stopped.

'Out you get,' said Phil, holding open the car door.

The girls climbed out and stood on the pavement, whilst Phil went ahead through the white gate, along the garden path to the front door. As she opened it, Charlie picked up the cases and carried them to the front door step.

'Come on, girls,' he said. 'In you come.' They walked into the hall. Charlie stopped inside, gave Phil a hug and a kiss and quickly went out, closing the front door behind him.

'Now,' said Phil. 'Come and see where you're going to sleep.'

She picked up their bags and they followed her upstairs.

'You'll need your beds early tonight, I should think,' she said as she opened a bedroom door.

'There you are — one bed each!'

'Lovely,' said Emma, as she looked round the pretty room admiringly.

'We share a bed at home,' said Fran timidly. Emma was glad to hear her talking at last. She had been so quiet all day.

'This will be a happy house to be in, until we go home,' thought Emma.

'Right next door is the bathroom,' said Phil, opening another door.

'A bathroom!' exclaimed Fran. 'We haven't got one at home.'

Emma suddenly felt embarrassed about that. 'But we *do* have baths,' she said, 'in the kitchen. We're not dirty.'

Phil gave them both a hug. 'I can see you're not dirty,' she said. 'Come on downstairs for supper. You must be starving.'

She led the way and they followed her into the kitchen, where lovely smells were coming out of the oven.

'Shepherd's pie,' she said. 'That's why I was a bit late coming to fetch you. Got that in the oven first.'

'Yummy,' chirped Fran. 'I *love* shepherd's pie.'

'Me too,' said Emma.

'What a lovely lady,' she thought. 'Late because she'd put supper in the oven first. Just like Mum.'

Emma felt really happy. Weren't they lucky? They sat round the table eating shepherd's pie, followed by trifle.

71

'Now,' said Phil. 'A quick wash and bed. You can have baths another night. You must be *so* tired now — and it's school tomorrow.'

'Oh yes,' said Emma. 'I've got a piece of paper, telling us where to go.' She went into the hall and pulled the card and piece of paper out of her pocket.

'Do you know where this is?' she asked Phil.

'Oh yes, no problem,' replied Phil. 'I'll come with you tomorrow. It's on my way to work. Then you might meet some other girls living out this way, so you can walk home with them.'

'Do you work?' asked Emma, surprised.

'Yes,' laughed Phil. 'I work in a shop, in the town — just part-time. My husband's in the army and doesn't get home very often.'

'Do you live here alone then?' asked Emma.

'Most of the time,' said Phil, 'which is why they made me take two evacuees.'

'They *made* you take us?' Emma was disturbed.

'Look – I shall *love* having you,' said Phil. 'Don't look so worried.' She chuckled. 'What's that card?'

'Oh yes,' said Emma. 'Can you write your name and address on it. Then we send it to Dad, so that he knows where we are.'

'Address it to him now,' said Phil. 'I'll fill in the other side, then we can drop it in the post box on the way to school.'

'Goody,' said Fran. 'He'll soon know where we are —then he can write and tell us where Mum and the others are.'

'Take about two weeks for the card to get to there,' said Emma sadly, as she addressed the card to Dad.

'I know,' said Phil. 'That's why we must get it off as quickly as possible.'

She piled the dirty plates onto the draining board.

'Ready?' she asked and led the way upstairs. Soon, they were tucked into their beds and fast asleep.

Chapter Nine

NEW HOME — NEW SCHOOL

A TAP at the door woke Emma in the morning.

'Time to get up girls,' called Phil. 'I've finished in the bathroom, so you can get washed.'

'Thank you,' said Emma, but Fran slept on. As she gently shook her, Emma heard Phil going downstairs.

'Come on Fran. Wake up. You're coming to school with me this morning.'

Drowsily, Fran rubbed her eyes and sat up.

'I'm going to the bathroom to wash,' said Emma, 'whilst you are waking up.'

'I'm coming to the bathroom with you,' said Fran and bounded out of bed. 'Want to see what you do.'

Emma was delighted that her sleepy-headed sister was so wide awake. They crept out of the bedroom door and into the bathroom. They looked at the wash basin.

'Two taps,' said Fran.

'One hot and one cold,' said Emma.

'How do you know which is which?' asked Fran.

'It tells you silly,' laughed Emma. 'H for hot and C for cold.'

'Oh yes,' said Fran as Emma cautiously turned the hot

tap. There was a sudden *Whoosh* over the bath and they both jumped.

'What's that?' whispered Fran in a scared voice. 'Have we broken something?'

Emma looked around carefully and saw blue flames inside the big white thing over the bath. She put her hand under the water coming out of the tap.

'It's hot!' she exclaimed. 'That thing must heat the water. Isn't it marvellous. No kettles!'

Having made the big discovery, they both quickly washed, cleaned their teeth, made the beds, got dressed, brushed their hair and went downstairs.

'Good morning,' called Phil from the kitchen. 'It's all ready. I suppose you like scrambled egg on toast?'

'Oh yes,' they both said.

'Scrummy,' added Fran.

'It's dried egg. I'm afraid,' said Phil. 'But it doesn't taste *too* bad — I've put a few things in to flavour it.'

75

Breakfast was a speedy affair and soon they were clearing away, with Phil washing whilst Emma and Fran dried. 'Amazing,' she thought. 'There's another of those hot water things over the sink down here.'

She did not say anything, or ask any questions, but she really *would* like to know what 'the thing' was called. Perhaps when they had been here a bit longer and knew Phil better, she could ask.

At last they were ready and walking down the front path, out of the white gate. A tall ginger-haired girl in Blankton School uniform was coming out of the house opposite, with two other girls and a boy.

'Mary,' called Emma.

Mary stopped. 'Emma, Fran — isn't that marvellous,' she said. 'We're neighbours!'

'Hello, you three,' said Phil. 'That's great. You can all go to school together. I'd forgotten that Pat and Annie went to the High School — and didn't even know you'd got an evacuee. Poor Benjie — all those girls!'

'That's fine, Phil,' said Pat. 'We can do this every day.'

'See you later then,' said Phil. 'I can go back and do a few more jobs before work. I'll post your card to Dad, Emma.'

'Must remember to post mine,' said Mary.

They waved goodbye to Phil and set off down the road.

'Benjie seems about the same age as Fran,' thought Emma. 'Annie's my size.'

'Pat's the same age as me,' said Mary. 'That's why her mother picked me.'

'Plus the red hair!' laughed Pat.

They certainly looked as if they could be sisters.

'How lucky that you live opposite us,' said Mary. 'What's it like there?'

'She's lovely,' said Emma, smiling happily. 'We're going to like it with Phil.'

By this time they had reached the end of the road and Pat led the way onto a rough footpath between a field and some woods.

'We take the short cut through here,' she said. 'Except when it's raining, then we'd get our shoes too muddy.'

As they filed behind each other, Emma thought, 'Just like the footpaths through the orchards and fields to the hop-gardens. Really makes me feel at home.'

Pat suddenly stopped and sniffed the air.

'The gippoes are back,' she whispered.

'The gypsies, you mean,' whispered Mary.

'Yes. They come back here and settle in for the winter,' explained Pat. 'A bit early this year.'

'P'raps they were near some bombing, or something,' said Mary 'and thought it would be safer here.'

They began to creep forward, peeping through the trees to see the gaily painted caravans parked in a clearing in the wood. Horses were tied to trees and a fire was smoking in the centre of the camp.

'I love it when the gypsies are here,' whispered Pat. 'Makes the walk to school much more interesting.'

'They're lucky,' Annie said to Emma. 'Travelling around all the time with their horses — not trapped in houses.'

A gypsy woman carried a pot to the fire and looked at them as they crept past. She had a scarf tied round her head and wore a long dress, covered with an apron. Her face was very brown, as if she spent a lot of time outside.

'Boo,' shouted a voice and a cheeky little gypsy boy jumped out of the trees in front of them.

'Come on you,' shouted the gypsy woman. 'Don't scare those young ladies.'

The boy rushed off giggling and a crowd of other boys came from behind the caravans to stare at the girls and Benjie as they went by.

'Hello,' called Pat and waved.

'Hi,' called the others.

'I think,' whispered Pat, 'if we're friendly to them — they'll be friendly to us.'

'We'd better hurry now,' said Annie, 'otherwise we'll be late and then there'll be trouble.'

They hurried along the path and out onto the road.

'Cross the road,' said Pat. 'That's our school over there. Benjie is at the prep. school next door.'

'Jolly convenient,' said Mary.

'What will I do?' Fran suddenly burst out. 'I go to a different school. Will they let me into yours?'

Mary took her hand. 'Don't worry,' she said. 'I'll find out.'

The girls went in through the school gate together and Benjie disappeared next door. Round in the playground, Miss Pring and Miss Plath stood together, watching the girls arrive.

'Blankton over here,' called Miss Pring.

'See you after school,' said Pat and she and Annie went to join their friends.

'Come with me,' said Mary and she took Fran to where the two teachers were standing.

'Please, Miss Plath,' she said. 'Emma is a new First Former and she has brought her younger sister, Fran, with her. When it's time to go in, where should Fran go?'

'Oh yes, I remember,' said Miss Plath, with a smile to Fran. 'Your sister spoke to me about you, the day before we left. You're eight, aren't you?'

'Yes,' said Fran shyly.

'Then I think you'd better join the Prep.* when the whistle blows,' said Miss Plath.

'That is,' Miss Pring interrupted, 'until a *local* school is found for you. We can't have just *anyone* in *our* school. Parents have to pay fees for the Prep.'

Fran looked ready to burst into tears. She was not used to unkind teachers. Miss Plath was concerned as she saw the unhappiness on the little girl's face, the anger in Mary's eyes and Emma's quivering lips. She took hold of Fran's hand.

'Come with me,' she said. 'I'll take you to find Miss Alexander, the Prep class teacher. You'll like her. She's nice.'

Fran looked happier as they walked away together.

Mary and Emma left Miss Pring standing there and went back towards the groups of girls without another word.

'I'm fuming,' said Mary, when they were out of ear-shot. 'That woman! I wished we'd dropped her off the train in London to be blown up by a bomb!'

'Thank goodness I wasn't alone with Fran,' said Emma, 'and that Miss Plath was there. I don't know how I'd cope with Miss Pring on my own.'

'Hope she's not your form mistress,' said Mary. 'She was mine when I was in the First Form. That's when I really began to hate her. I don't hate many people — but *her*, I can't stand.'

Emma began to worry again. She certainly had not thought about a form mistress and if it was Miss Pring, she knew she would be really scared.

'The one *good* thing,' she thought, 'we've got a *lovely* billet. Phil is so nice and kind.'

*Preparatory or Junior class

A whistle blew and the High School girls disappeared. Miss Pring blew her whistle.

'Line up — form order,' she called. '6th, 5th, 4th, 3rd, 2nd, 1st — and Prep.' She indicated where they should stand.

'I'm with the 4th Form,' said Mary. 'See you later.'

Emma went across to the 1st Form line.

'Hello,' said Peggy. 'I'm so glad to see you.'

'And me,' said Emma and looked around the group. 'I don't know anyone else.'

Chapter Ten

ALPHA AND OMEGA

'YOUR form mistresses will join you,' announced Miss Pring, 'and show you to the rooms the High School is so kindly letting us use.'

Emma did not normally bite her nails, but she found herself chewing away as she anxiously waited to see which teacher would come to them. She saw Fran chatting to two girls in the Prep, so she knew that she was settled for the time being.

'Wouldn't it be *awful* if we got Pringle?' whispered Peggy. 'She was Eileen's form mistress in the first year and she was *beastly*.'

'Mary told me,' whispered Emma. 'Pray hard Peggy. *Very* hard.' She shut her eyes, because she could not bear to watch any longer, waiting to see which of the teachers turned in their direction. She heard footsteps coming across the playground.

'Open your eyes, Emma,' whispered Peggy.

'Tell me — tell me,' said Emma, her eyes still screwed up.

'It's Miss Plath,' laughed Peggy.

'Thank goodness,' breathed Emma. 'With her as our

form mistress and Phil as our hostess, I think it's going to be fine.'

Miss Plath led the way across the playground to some wooden huts. She opened the door of one of them and they filed in to find old desks, set out in rows, waiting for them.

'Sit anywhere,' she said, 'then I'll call the register and see who we've got.'

Emma and Peggy made for the back and took desks next to each other. From there, they were able to watch the other girls.

'How do we know who are the new ones, like us?' whispered Emma.

'Those who talk posh were in the Prep,' Peggy whispered back. 'We'll have to go to speech training classes to make us sound like Blankton girls.'

'What?' Emma could hardly believe what she was hearing.

'Quiet girls,' said Miss Plath. She had a blank piece of paper in front of her. 'Today we will *make* the register. We really have no record of who came with us and who remained at home.

'Stand up if your surname begins with A.' No-one moved. 'Right — B,' she went on and Emma stood.

'BA,' said Miss Plath. Emma put up her hand.

'BARTON,' she said 'Emma Barton.'

Miss Plath smiled. 'You'll be the first on the register then.'

She continued through the alphabet and reached X. Peggy still had not stood up.

'Anybody else?' asked Miss Plath.

Peggy stood up. 'Yes me, Miss Plath,' she said.

'It looks as if you will be last on the register. We'll need to call you two Alpha and Omega — first and last,' she said with a laugh. 'What's your surname then?'

'YORK Miss Plath,' Peggy said. 'Margaret York.'

'Eileen's sister?' asked Miss Plath.

'Yes, that's right,' replied Peggy. She continued shyly, 'Everyone calls me Peggy, not Margaret.'

Miss Plath smiled. 'That's fine,' she said. 'We'll call you whatever you're happiest with — but we'd better put Margaret in the register.'

'Yes, Miss Plath,' said Peggy and sat down.

'Now timetable,' went on Miss Plath. 'I'll write it on the board and you copy it down. Will you give out the paper please, Geraldine.'

The day passed very quickly until the final bell rang. The girls pushed pencils and note-books into their desks and made for the door.

''Bye Alpha — 'Bye Omega,' called some, as they disappeared in different directions. Peggy and Emma laughed.

'Nice to have nick-names,' said Emma. 'Even if they can't remember our real names, they'll remember those.'

'We'll soon be down to Alph and Ome,' said Peggy with a grin. 'There's Eileen. Better go. See you tomorrow' — and she ran across to her sister.

Emma looked for Fran and began to get worried when she saw none of the other little ones around. She ran across to Eileen and Peggy as they left the playground.

'Is Mary around? Where are the Prep girls?' she asked anxiously.

'It's O.K.,' said Eileen. 'Mary went off to find Fran as soon as we got out. Thought she might be frightened on her own. Look, here they come.'

A relieved Emma saw them coming across the playground.

'Thanks, Eileen,' she said. ' 'Bye Ome.'

Peggy gave a giggle.

'What's that?' asked Eileen, as they walked off. Emma saw Peggy giggling as they made their way home. She turned and ran to meet Mary and Fran.

'Thanks, Mary,' she said. 'I was worried about where to find Fran.'

'Thought Fran would be worried about where to find *us*,' laughed Mary. 'Come on. Let's go and look for the others.'

They walked round to the front of the school and saw Pat, Annie and Benjie waiting.

'How did it go?' asked Pat.

'Strange sort of day,' replied Mary. 'We've got time-tables and form mistresses. We know who came away — and who didn't. We've had some lessons. Not sure that we've actually learned anything. The good news — no homework,' she finished with a chuckle.

'Same here,' said the others.

'I think the teachers have had so much to do, that they really haven't had time to think about work,' said Pat.

'We weren't supposed to start for another week, anyway,' said Mary. 'If it hadn't been for evacuation, I would have still been apple-picking and Emma and Fran hop-picking.'

'Today was our right day,' said Pat. 'P'raps we go back earlier than you because there's no fruit and hops around here to pick.'

'Dunno,' said Mary.

They were now walking along the path between the fields and the wood. Pat stopped talking and slowed down.

'Nearly at the gippoes camp,' she whispered.

'Boo'

'Boo'

'Boo'

'Boo'

Gypsy boys poked their heads from behind the trees to frighten them — and then ran away giggling.

'Don't they go to school?' asked Emma.

'Shouldn't think so,' said Pat. 'They're always moving on.'

'Lucky things,' said Annie.

'Well, how do they learn to read and write?' asked Emma.

'They don't,' said Mary.

'So it means the've always got to be gypsies, whether they want to, or not,' commented Emma.

'Well — yes,' replied Pat. 'They earn their money on the farms in the summer and autumn, and selling wooden pegs in the winter.'

'They make the pegs themselves,' joined in Annie.

85

'Sometimes you can see them, sitting around here, scratching and cutting away with knives.'

By this time, they had reached the end of the path and were back home.

' 'Bye,' said Emma to the others, as she and Fran opened the gate and walked along the path to the front door. It opened before they could knock. Phil's smiling face greeted them.

'Hello,' she said. 'I was looking out for you. Bet you could do with a drink.'

She closed the door behind them and they followed her into the kitchen. A teapot, mugs and biscuits were set out on the table. Soon, they were drinking, eating and chatting, telling Phil about the gypsies, school, Miss Pring and Miss Plath.

'She sounds a real "so and so",' said Phil about Miss Pring. 'I remember teachers just like that. Trouble is, they're *so* horrid, that you never forget them — and they put you off school.'

There was a knock at the door. Phil went and soon re-appeared with Charlie.

'Hi, girls,' he said. 'Thought we could go out and get fish and chips for supper.'

'Love–ly,' said Fran.

'Oh yes,' said Emma, thinking — fish and chips are jolly expensive. P'raps he means fish and chips for him and Phil and just chips for us. That's what they did at home.

'I've got the car, so thought you'd like a ride to the fish and chip shop,' he said.

Fish and chips — and a ride in a car! They were *so* lucky.

'Have a cup of tea first,' said Phil, pouring it out for him. 'I don't know where you get all that petrol from. It's supposed to be rationed.'

Charlie wagged his finger at her. 'Don't ask,' he said. 'There are ways of getting things, even if there is a war on.'

Soon they were ready to go out and Emma and Fran were very thrilled to climb into the back seat of the car. They sat there, feeling very grand, wishing that some of their friends would come along, so that they could wave.

All too soon they were at the fish and chip shop.

'Want to come in?' asked Charlie. 'Tell me what sort of fish you like.'

'So we *are* going to have fish,' thought Emma.

They climbed out and went into the shop.

'Hi, Charlie,' said the large fish and chip man. 'What d'you want then?'

'Five pieces of fish — and chips,' replied Charlie.

'What sort?' asked the fish and chip man.

'Well, cod for me,' said Charlie. 'Phil, what about you and the girls?'

'Rock,' said Phil. 'What about you Emma — and Fran?'

'We'll have rock,' said Emma, not at all sure about what she was ordering, but hoping that it was not *too* hard.

The fish and chip shop man counted out the three pieces of rock and three bags of chips.

'Two cod for you, Charlie?' he asked.

'S'right,' said Charlie, feeling in his pocket for money.

'*Two* pieces of fish,' thought Emma. 'Five altogether. What a lot of money that will cost.'

The rest of the evening past very happily and as she and Fran got ready for bed, Emma said, 'We are so lucky to be living here. I never thought evacuation, away from Mum and Dad, could be as happy as this.'

Chapter Eleven

PRINGLE AND THE BROW-W-N COW-W

WHEN Miss Plath took the register at school the next day, there were a few grins from the other girls as they remembered Alpha and Omega. They had just reached the end, when Miss Pring came into the classroom.

She had a word with Miss Plath and then said, 'Stand up, all new girls.' Peggy and Emma stood, with about ten of the others.

'Hands up scholarship girls,' she continued. Six hands, including Peggy's and Emma's, went up.

'Right,' she said. 'Speech training for all new girls at lunch time today. You may not all need it. The *scholarship* girls *certainly* will,' and she glared across at Emma.

Emma felt herself blush as she remembered Miss Pring's correction of 'oppin' to *h*opping. She dreaded the thought of speech training with Miss Pring.

'Funny,' she thought. 'I'd never thought about speaking badly — I sound just the same as my friends and family. What's wrong with that?'

'Sit,' said Miss Pring and turned to have another word with Miss Plath.

'This'll be *awful*,' whispered Peggy.

'Will we sound posh when she's finished with us?' asked Emma, in a *very* quiet voice.

'Yes,' Peggy replied. 'We'll be like Eileen — talk posh for school and ordinary at home!'

Miss Pring left the room.

'Ready girls,' said Miss Plath. 'Real work today and if you look at your timetables, you will see it's Maths. I am your Maths teacher.'

They worked solidly all through the morning, with subject mistresses coming and going. All too soon, the mid-day bell rang and the girls filed out for school lunch. Those who had to go on to speech training stayed together and rushed through their meal, so as not to be late for Miss Pring. It was going to be bad enough without *that*.

To her relief, Emma discovered that no-one was looking forward to this session. When they finally arrived at Miss Pring's classroom and filed silently in, she was waiting for them.

'Good afternoon girls,' she said. 'Push back the desks and stand in a line.'

They stood facing her.

'Repeat,' she said.

'How–w Now–w Brow–w–n Cow–w.'

The girls repeated, copying her as best they could.

'New girls — non-scholarship,' she said. 'Stand in a group together at this end.' She indicated the space nearest the door and they reshuffled in the line.

'Repeat again,' she said.

'How–w Now–w Brow–w–n Cow–w.'

Beautifully, perfectly, the non-scholarship girls did as they were told and she walked down the line, listening acutely.

'You may go,' she said and they filed out of the door.

Emma felt her heart sink. Only *six* of them for Miss Pring to be unkind to.

'Now scholarship girls,' she said. 'Let's hear you.'

'How-w Now-w Brow-w-n Cow-w.'

They dutifully repeated the meaningless words, whilst she walked along the short line listening.

She faced them. 'Kentish. Typically Kentish,' she said scornfully. 'There is an 'e' for egg in *every* word. Kent *might* be the Garden of England, but do *not* let the chicken lay their eggs in your spoken language.'

Emma felt herself going very red, because she did not *quite* understand what Miss Pring was getting at and knew, that if she said the words again, they would not sound any different.

Miss Pring was still talking. 'I do *not* want to hear — He-oo Ne-oo Bre-oon Ke-oo, through flattened lips. I want nice round sounds.

'Listen.

'How-w Now-w Brow-w-n Cow-w.

'Repeat.'

They tried. They really tried to please her, but from the look on her face, they knew they were not succeeding. Fortunately, the bell rang.

'Time for afternoon lessons,' she announced. 'I want you to practise *every* day — *every* day and return next week at this same time. I *hope* to hear great improvements.'

She marched out of the room. The girls stood still, upset and angry.

'Fancy attacking us like that,' burst out Peggy. 'Looking down her snotty, snobbish nose at us, just because we don't come from posh homes and have parents who don't sound like her!'

Emma was glad that Peggy was angry. She felt like

crying, but was now filling herself with the courage to be angry instead.

'I know now how Eileen felt, when it happened to her,' went on Peggy, as they walked back to their classroom, 'Dad laughed at her posh new voice, but Mum was upset and hardly dares to open her mouth when she goes to Blankton. Afraid Pringle will grab her!'

Peggy and Emma settled themselves at the back of the classroom, ready for afternoon lessons. Emma's mind kept drifting off to Miss Pring's unkind remarks and she felt deeply unhappy. She shook herself.

'Stop it,' she silently told herself. 'You are lucky. You have Peggy as a friend and she is in the same boat — but *she* is angry, *not* upset. You're lucky. You're living with a lovely lady like Phil. Stop being miserable. It could be *much* worse.' (Fortunately, she did not know it was going to get much worse.)

Having given herself a good telling-off, she was able to concentrate for the rest of the afternoon, until the bell rang and she was able to escape from the classroom to join Mary and Fran.

As they walked home, Emma was able to tell Mary about the dreadful speech training session.

'I know,' said Mary. 'I've been through it — eggs and all.'

'What's that about eggs?' called Pat, who was walking ahead with Annie and Benjie.

'Just talking about where our Kentish chicken lay their eggs,' replied Mary, with a grin to Emma.

'Boo'

'Boo'

'Boo'

It was the gypsy boys popping out again, almost as if they had been waiting for them. Their mother shouted from a caravan and the boys ran off giggling.

'Lucky things,' said Emma. 'No school. No Miss Pring.'

'Wish they'd have a go at frightening her!' laughed Pat.

As they turned the corner and approached Phil's white gate, Emma saw an ARP lady, standing outside. Their cases were beside her and their coats were over her arm.

'Are you the Barton girls?' she asked.

'Yes,' replied Emma, wondering what she could be wanting.

'I am afraid that you will not be staying with Mrs Philips from now on,' she said. 'We have found another billet for you.'

'But — but,' Emma was flabbergasted. 'Doesn't — Phil want us any more?' she stammered out.

'Oh yes,' said the lady, stiffly. 'She wants *you*, but *we* do not want *her*.'

'But – but — she's a *lovely* lady,' burst out Emma, hardly able to believe what she was hearing.

'That's as may be,' said the ARP lady. 'I have your cases. Come with me.'

The others had been watching from across the road, and hearing Emma's outburst, Mary came across.

'Is anything wrong?' she asked.

Emma burst into tears and cried, 'They want to take us away from Phil's and send us somewhere else.'

'Why?' asked Mary.

'*We* have decided,' said the lady.

'I think,' said Mary, pulling herself to her full height so that she was as tall as the ARP lady, 'we will need to consult our headmistress.'

'You will need to do *what*?' said the ARP lady indignantly. 'It is *nothing* to do with her.'

'I am afraid it is,' said Mary. 'Our parents have trusted her with our care and so, before Emma and Fran move, I think we should go and see her.'

It was the ARP lady's turn to be speechless.

'Take your coats,' Mary said. 'It looks like rain. I'll fetch mine. Pat knows where Miss Cannon lives, so we'll go and see her.'

The ARP lady realised it was no good protesting. Mary was obviously in charge. She picked up the two cases.

'I will take these to the Church Hall,' she said. 'On your return, kindly come and tell me what your headmistress says.' She turned to go and added, mysteriously, 'I *think* you will find that she knows all about it.'

Emma and Fran miserably put their coats on and went across the road to where Pat and Annie were still waiting. Mary explained what had happened.

'I think you're right to see your Head,' agreed Pat. 'I'll come with you, to make sure you don't get lost.'

'Me too,' said Annie. 'We'll tell Mum and collect our coats.'

Emma and Fran stood on the pavement waiting. Cautiously, Emma looked across the road. She saw the net curtain move and Phil waved, then blew them a kiss. Emma waved back.

'Blow Phil a kiss,' she said to Fran, hardly able to keep back the tears.

'Saying goodbye *again*,' thought Emma desperately. It seemed like a bad dream and she would either wake up in her bed at home, or sitting proudly on the back seat of Charlie's car.

Chapter 12

'YOU'VE GOT TO GO' — AGAIN

EMMA was feeling very upset as she and Fran walked with Annie along the unfamiliar roads leading to Miss Cannon's billet. Mary and Pat were behind, talking quietly together.

A thought struck Emma and she turned round to Mary. 'What about the cards?' she said. 'We've sent the cards to Dad giving Phil's address. He'll send that on to Mum and Bill — and it will all be wrong. We *still* won't know where anyone is.' She was ready to cry.

'Lost,' she thought. 'I really feel lost, cut off from my family.'

'Don't worry,' said Mary. 'We'll ask Miss Cannon.'

'Round here,' said Pat. 'This is her road.'

The houses were very large, with long drives leading up to the front doors.

'The Firs,' said Pat, stopping outside a beautiful brick house, covered in ivy. The drive leading to it had lawns on each side, with beds of flowering roses. 'This is where Miss Cannon is staying.'

They all crunched along the gravel drive and Mary rang the door bell. A tall lady answered.

'Please may we see Miss Cannon?' Mary asked.

'What, *all* of you?' asked the lady, in a surprised voice.

'Well, no,' said Mary awkwardly. 'It's Emma who really needs to see her.'

'Which one of you is Emma?' asked the lady.

Emma stepped forward. 'I am,' she said, feeling very nervous.

'Then you come in,' said the lady, 'and the others can wait quietly out here.'

'May I come with her?' asked Mary, knowing that Emma would be terrified.

'There is no need,' replied the lady. 'If Miss Cannon wants to speak to you, we will come out and fetch you.'

She ushered Emma into a spacious hall, with a beautifully polished wooden floor, then closed the front door firmly behind them.

'Follow me,' she said, going over to a door further down the hall. She tapped gently.

'Come in,' called Miss Cannon.

'You have a visitor,' said the tall lady.

Emma could feel her legs shaking as she went in through the open door towards Miss Cannon, who was sitting behind a table piled with papers. The lady went out and closed the door.

'Good evening,' said Miss Cannon, peering at her over her glasses. 'I believe you are a new girl.'

'Yes, Miss Cannon,' replied Emma shyly. 'I'm Emma Barton and I've just started at Blankton.'

'Well, Emma,' continued Miss Cannon. 'At Blankton, girls *never* wear a coat without wearing gloves. *You* are wearing a raincoat. *Where* are your gloves?'

Emma felt her face going bright pink and her knees shaking so hard, that she was sure Miss Cannon would hear them knocking.

'I–I–d–didn't br–bring any, Miss Cannon,' she stammered.

'Then Emma, you must *get* some,' said Miss Cannon in a firm voice. 'And do *not* wear your coat again until you have.'

'No, Miss Cannon. Yes, Miss Cannon,' said Emma nervously.

'Now,' said Miss Cannon, in a slightly kinder voice, 'What have you come to see me about so urgently?'

It took all of Emma's courage to open her mouth again and talk to this strict headmistress. She wanted to turn and rush out of the door.

'Well, Miss Cannon,' she managed to get out. 'When we got home from school, an ARP lady said we couldn't stay with Phil — Mrs Philips — any more. We had to go somewhere else.' Emma felt her lips, as as well as her legs, trembling. She was afraid she was going to cry.

'That is quite right,' said Miss Cannon. 'It has been decided that Mrs Philips is not a suitable person to have Blankton girls in her house.'

'But she's lovely,' burst out Emma. 'She's made us *very* happy.'

'*We* will decide if she is right,' said Miss Cannon stiffly. 'I am sure your parents would *not* approve of her.'

'But they would,' pleaded Emma.

'I'm sorry,' said Miss Cannon firmly, 'but you are *not* going back there. Another billet has been found for you and your sister. That is all. You may go.'

There was one more thing Emma had to say.

'Please Miss Cannon,' she pleaded. 'What about Dad? We've sent him a card with Phil's address on. It'll be *ages* before he and Mum know where we are, if we have to move.'

Emma burst into tears. It really was all too much.

Miss Cannon softened a little. 'Leave it to me,' she said. 'I am going back to Kenabury at the weekend and will ask Mr King, the school attendance officer to contact your father.'

'Thank you, Miss Cannon,' breathed Emma through her tears. 'Mr King knows Dad and I'm *sure* he'll give him the message.'

Feeling a little better, Emma left the room, crossed the hall, opened the heavy front door and joined the others in the drive.

Mary looked anxious. 'How did you get on?' she asked and Emma burst into tears again.

'Let's get out of here,' said Pat and they crunched down the drive.

'We've got to move,' sobbed Emma. 'They don't approve of Phil — but she's *lovely*.'

Fran started to cry and they all stood outside in the road, looking very worried.

'*Why* don't they approve?' asked Mary, looking at Pat for an answer.

'I don't really know,' said Pat, with an embarrassed look. 'It might be that her husband's away in the Army and Charlie is her boyfriend.'

She and Mary exchanged glances. Emma, Fran and Annie still looked puzzled.

'Don't worry about that,' said Mary hurriedly. 'Did she tell you where you're going?'

'No,' said Emma dismally. 'We'd better find that ARP lady again and let her take us to the new billet.'

As they set off down the road, none of them were feeling very cheerful. Emma looked at Mary's hands.

'Mary,' she said quietly. 'Have you got any gloves?'

Mary started to giggle. 'No,' she said. 'I forgot them. Gloves — flippin' gloves.'

Emma felt better. 'That's where Miss Cannon started,' she said. '*Where* are your gloves?' It was such a good imitation, that the others started giggling.

'I could kick myself,' said Mary. 'I should have known what she'd say.'

'Well,' said Emma, 'I shan't wear this coat again, however cold or wet it is, until I get some gloves. Can't imagine where from ...' Her voice trailed off as she thought of Dad searching for gloves. She then remembered that all of her gloves were brown! They would not look right with a navy blue raincoat.

'There are *important* things to think about,' thought

Emma, 'and here am I worried about silly old gloves — and it's not even cold!'

By this time they had reached the end of their road.

'Shall we go straight to the Church Hall?' asked Pat.

'Can we,' asked Emma hesitantly, 'go past Phil's house, so that I can thank her and say goodbye?'

'Of course we can,' said Pat, 'and I'll pop in and tell Mum what's happening.'

They reached the white gate. Emma and Fran went up to the front door and knocked. They heard footsteps and Phil opened it. When she saw them her face lit up.

'Can you stay?' she asked eagerly.

'No,' said Emma, feeling awful. 'They won't let us. But *we* want to. You've been lovely — and thank you.'

Phil gave her a big hug, then bent down to Fran.

'I'm sorry,' she said. 'I'm sorry. It was great having you here. I hope you'll be happy where you're going. I *love kids*,' she finished fiercely.

She hugged them both again and took them to the front gate, where Pat, Mary and Annie were waiting.

'I hope you'll be happy,' she said again. 'It's been lovely having you.'

Chapter Thirteen

UNHAPPY — AND HUNGRY

WHEN they reached the Church Hall, the ARP lady was waiting for them.

'So you've decided to do as you're told, have you?' she said. 'I *knew* your headmistress wouldn't let you stay with that woman.'

'Where are you taking them to?' asked Pat.

'Just around the corner into The Gardens,' the ARP lady replied, 'to stay with Mr and Mrs Crick.'

'Look,' said Pat to Emma, 'meet us outside the Church Hall tomorrow morning at half past eight. We can all go to school together.'

'Thanks,' said Emma. 'I was wondering if we'd get lost.'

'Say goodbye to your friends,' said the ARP lady. 'Mrs Crick will be expecting us.'

' 'Bye,' said the girls, as Mary, Pat and Annie left the Church Hall.

The ARP lady picked up the cases and Emma and Fran followed her out. Down the road they went, round the corner, into a very nice tree-lined road. The houses were quite new and they all had tidy, little front gardens.

'P'raps it'll be alright,' thought Emma hopefully.

101

At number thirty-four the ARP lady stopped.

'This is Mrs Crick's,' she said and went up to the front door. She rang the bell and footsteps could be heard in the hall. A child cried and a fair-haired lady, holding a little girl, opened the door.

'Hello, Mrs Crick,' said the ARP lady. 'I've brought your evacuees — Emma and Fran Barton.'

'They'd better come in then,' said Mrs Crick, without a smile.

Emma's heart sank. 'This lady doesn't want us,' she thought.

They stepped inside. The ARP lady handed in their cases and the door was shut after her. Mrs Crick put her little girl down.

'Take off your shoes,' she said to Emma and Fran. 'You must never walk into my house with your shoes on. You'll spoil the carpets.'

They both bent down and undid their shoes.

'Give them to me. I'll put them by the back door,' said Mrs Crick. 'When you've unpacked your cases, you can put your slippers on.'

'We haven't got any slippers,' blurted out Emma.

'Then you'll have to go around in your socks until you get some,' said Mrs Crick, without a smile.

'First gloves — now slippers!' thought Emma miserably, wondering where the coupons *and* the money were coming from to get them.

'Carry your cases upstairs,' said Mrs Crick. 'I'll show you to your room.' She went on ahead with the the little girl.

Emma took her own case and saw Fran struggling with her bag. A bedroom door stood open and Mrs Crick indicated that this was to be their room. There was a double bed, two chairs, a table and a wardrobe.

'You will have your meals downstairs in the kitchen, but I shall expect you to spend the rest of your time up here,' she said. 'My husband and I do not want to be pestered with two young strangers in our living rooms.'

Emma felt her heart sink. This was *terrible*. Never had she felt so unwanted. Why did the ARP lady and Miss Cannon think that Mum and Dad would prefer Mrs Crick to Phil? Emma knew they would love Phil and hate Mrs Crick.

'The bathroom is next door. Always leave it clean and tidy when you've finished,' she said. 'And do not use too much hot water. It costs money.'

'It gets worse,' thought Emma.

'Have you had your tea?' asked Mrs Crick.

'Well–no,' said Emma, not sure whether she should have lied and said 'yes'.

'Oh,' said Mrs Crick, sounding surprised. 'I *quite* thought you would have had tea by this time. I'll make you a few sandwiches and give you a call when they're ready.'

She left the room, with her little girl still in her arms, shutting the door behind her. Emma sat heavily on the bed and looked at Fran.

'Oh Fran,' she said miserably, 'I don't think we're going to be very happy here.'

'Why can't we go home?' sobbed Fran and flung her arms round Emma's neck.

Emma found herself crying too. 'We can't go home and we can't go back to Phil's,' she said in despair. 'Why do some grown-ups like making children unhappy?'

They sat on the bed together feeling helpless and hopeless.

'We're going to see a lot of this room,' said Emma, 'so we'd better start liking it.'

'P'raps,' said Fran, 'it'll be better for us up here on our own, than downstairs with *her.*'

'Poor little girl,' said Emma. 'Fancy having her for a mum!'

'She didn't even tell us the baby's name,' said Fran. 'Funny that. People usually do — at least, the people we know do.'

'We don't know anybody like Mrs Crick,' said Emma. 'P'raps Fanny Farmer was like her when she was young. *She* doesn't like children — well, not us and our friends.'

A voice called up from below.

'The sandwiches are ready. Come down now.'

They wiped their eyes, blew their noses and tidied their hair, before going downstairs. Carefully, they walked on the hall carpet to the kitchen.

'Have you washed your hands?' was Mrs Crick's greeting.

'Oh, no,' said Emma. 'We forgot.'

'You'd better go back and do it then,' went on Mrs Crick and silently the girls climbed the stairs again to the bathroom.

'Better use cold water,' whispered Emma, 'otherwise *that* will be wrong.'

With clean hands, they went back down and once more approached the kitchen door.

'Come in,' said Mrs Crick and they entered a spotlessly clean kitchen. It was so clean, that it did not look as if it was ever used.

'Sit down,' she said, indicating the kitchen table. A small plate of sandwiches stood in the middle, with two glasses of orange squash.

'You can eat those whilst I go and bath Shirley,' said Mrs Crick, picking up the little girl and going out into the hall.

'Clear your things away onto the draining board when you've finished,' she called, as she went upstairs.

It did not take them long to silently eat the sandwiches and drink the squash. They did as they were told and carried the plates and glasses from the table to the draining board, then sat down again on their chairs — and waited.

'Do you think there's anything else to eat?' whispered Fran. 'I'm *hungry*.'

'So am I,' Emma whispered back. 'Let's see when she comes down.'

They sat, listening for the footsteps on the stairs. At last they heard them and then Mrs Crick returned to the kitchen with Shirley.

'So you've finished,' she said. 'What are you waiting here for? You can go to your room.'

'Thank you, Mrs Crick,' said Emma, not knowing what else to say.

'Thank you,' said Fran.

'Good night,' said Mrs Crick. 'I'll call you at quarter past seven tomorrow morning.'

'Good night,' said the girls to her.

'Night, night Shirley,' Emma said, with a little wave. Shirley smiled, as if pleased to be included at last. They climbed the stairs to the bedroom and once again, plonked down on the bed, looking helplessly at each other.

'It's still light,' said Fran. 'What's the time?'

Emma looked at her watch. 'Not quite seven o'clock,' she said. 'Not bedtime yet.'

'What can we do?' asked Fran. 'We can't just *sit* here.' She looked ready to cry again.

'It's going to be awful — and *every* night,' said Emma. 'What about Saturdays and Sundays? Does she expect us just to stay up here all the time?'

'Wish we could run away,' said Fran pouting, which was quite unlike her.

'Well, we can't do that,' said Emma, with a faint smile. 'We'd get lost — *then* what would Mum and Dad say?'

There was a sharp knock at the bedroom door and a man's voice called, 'Can I come in?'

Emma and Fran jumped up from the bed and went to the door.

'Yes,' said Emma. 'Please do.'

The door opened and the man said, 'I'm Mr Crick. Thought I would come and introduce myself.' He put out his hand and shook first Emma's hand, then Fran's

'I've just come home from work,' he explained. 'The wife told me you were here. Brought you up some games. Thought you might be bored with nothing to do.' He handed them Snakes and Ladders and Draughts.

'Keep them up here,' he said. 'I used to have a boy once. Would have been about your age.' He looked at Emma. 'He and his mother were very ill. Lost them both. Miss them a lot.'

'Are you coming down?' called Mrs Crick. 'Your supper's ready.'

'I'll have to go,' said Mr Crick and went out, shutting the door behind him. Emma and Fran looked at each other.

'That was nice of him,' said Fran.

'Bet *she* didn't like it,' said Emma.

'P'raps it won't be as bad when he's at home,' said Fran hopefully.

'He's afraid of her Fran, can't you see?' said Emma dismally. 'At least it's not just us — and *he's* got her for life, so has Shirley.'

'Not us,' said Fran. 'We've got our own Mum and Dad to go back to.'

'One day,' said Emma. 'One day.'

106

Chapter Fourteen

YET ANOTHER CHANGE

Long after Fran had fallen asleep, Emma tossed and turned. She heard Mrs Crick bring Shirley up and put her to bed. She heard Mr and Mrs Crick climb the stairs, use the bathroom, then close their bedroom door. Quietly, very quietly, she started to cry.

'Evacuation is bad enough,' she thought. 'Leaving Dad. Not knowing where Mum and the others are. Miss Pring — and *now* Mrs Crick.' These miserable thoughts kept chasing round in her mind — and the tears kept falling.

She *knew* she had to sleep, otherwise she would be useless at school tomorrow, but how do you sleep when you have no happy thoughts inside your head?

No happy thoughts? She decided she *must* be wrong and decided that, instead of counting sheep, or whatever you are supposed to count when you can't sleep, she would count the *good* things that were happening to her. Were there any?

Fran, Mary, Miss Plath, Peggy. The walk to school with Pat. . . .

The next thing she knew was a tapping at the door.

'Time to get up,' announced Mrs Crick's unwelcome voice.

Emma rubbed her eyes.

'Thank you,' she said sleepily.

'You may use the bathroom,' called the voice. 'Don't use too much hot water and clean up after you.'

'Yes, Mrs Crick,' replied Emma dismally. 'What a way to start the day,' she thought.

She shook Fran and speedily they got ready for school. Breakfast was waiting for them — a few cornflakes in a dish, covered with a little milk. It did not take long to eat. Their shoes were at the back door and they carried them through the hall to the front door, before putting them on. As they left the house, Emma breathed a sigh of relief.

'Thank goodness to get away,' she said.

'You all right?' asked Fran.

'Yes, Why?' replied Emma, trying to keep the irritation out of her voice.

'Your eyes look a bit funny,' said Fran.

'Nothing wrong,' said Emma. 'Didn't sleep very well.'

By this time they had reached the Church Hall. The others were waiting for them, reading a large notice.

Welcome Party
for
Evacuees,
— Hosts, Hostesses and local children
invited as well.
Saturday afternoon, 3.30 pm
Tea and biscuits.

Pat turned as she heard them coming.

'That's nice,' she said. 'A party. Let's all come.'

'Oh yes,' said Emma. 'Anything to get away.'

Mary looked at her sharply. 'Is it so bad?' she asked,

noticing Emma's swollen eyes and pale cheeks. 'You don't look as if you slept very well.'

'She's horrid,' burst out Fran. 'Absolutely horrid.'

'Oh, I'm sorry,' said Pat with a troubled look on her face. 'Mum was worried when she heard what had happened. She knows the Cricks.'

'Thought you would have been *much* happier staying with Phil,' said Annie.

'Oh! We would, we would,' said Emma on the verge of tears again. 'It's like living with Pringle — so you can guess how bad it is.'

'Another Pringle!' gasped Mary. 'You poor things.'

By this time, they were walking along the path by the side of the gypsy camp. Smoke was rising from the fire and a pot was boiling away.

'Smells good,' said Pat.

'I'm *hungry*,' wailed Fran.

'Oh gosh — isn't she feeding you properly either?' asked Mary.

'Well, it's such a tiny little bit, that you're nearly as hungry when you get up, as when you sat down,' explained Emma. She went on to tell them about the rules — staying in the bedroom and only coming out for meals.

There were gasps of surprise and murmurs of sympathy.

'Thank goodness to have friends to talk to,' thought Emma.

Pat was fumbling in her pocket. 'Goody,' she said, fishing out a halfpenny. 'Thought I'd got one. After school, instead of going straight home, we'll go to the biscuit factory.'

'They sell big bags of broken biscuits for a ha'penny,' joined in Annie.

'We'll fill you up with biscuits,' said Pat. 'Can't let you starve.'

'Sounds marvellous,' said Emma, feeling much better.

110

'Isn't that good Fran?' Fran's face looked happier than it had since hearing the news about leaving Phil's.

'Right, see you out here after school,' said Pat, as they came to the spot where they separated and went their different ways.

Emma joined Peggy in the classroom.

'What's up with you?' asked Peggy.

Emma began to tell her the sad tale. By the time she had finished, most of the girls in the class were crowding round.

'You poor things.'

'Poor old Alph.'

'Hope it doesn't happen to me,' they were saying when Miss Plath's voice interrupted them.

'Sit girls,' she said. 'Register.'

When she had checked that they had all arrived, she said, 'Hands up those who have brothers at Blankton Boys.'

Emma's hand shot up, plus three or four others.

'Blankton Boys *are* in Reading,' Miss Plath told them with a smile. 'And it has been decided that your brothers will be brought here on Saturday morning to meet you.'

'Marvellous,' breathed Emma. 'We're going to see Bill on Saturday.'

'The staff of both schools thought that it would be helpful for brothers and sisters to be in touch again,' Miss Plath went on.

'One last thing — did any of you bring younger sisters with you?'

Emma put her hand up again.

'Yes, of course,' said Miss Plath. 'I remember. It seems a very long time ago that we stood in the school playground and you asked me if she could come. Will you come to see me here at dinner time?'

'Yes, Miss Plath,' said Emma, wondering what else was going to happen. Nothing seemed secure any more.

'Now,' said Miss Plath. 'I think it's time for maths.'

When the bell rang at the end of the morning, Emma waited to see Miss Plath. She felt happier about this, than going to Miss Pring for speech training yesterday.

Other girls, unknown to Emma, came into the room.

'I s'pose they've all got sisters here,' she thought.

Miss Plath came in. 'Sit down, girls,' she said.

'The staff here have been discussing your younger sisters.' Her voice was kind and gentle as she continued. 'There are some problems. The school agreed they could come away with you and be billeted with you. *But*, they did *not* agree that they could join Blankton Prep class without paying fees.'

Her face showed that she was concerned about the news she was passing on.

'The evacuation happened in such a hurry, as you all know, that no-one really thought about school fees — and things like that.

'Talks have been held with the Church of England school in Wood Lane. They have said that they are happy to take your younger sisters into the school from next Monday. Are there any questions?'

The 'big' sisters were silent. 'Stunned, I expect,' thought Emma. 'Poor Fran — more changes.'

'If any of you have problems with the new arrangements,' said Miss Plath, 'please let me know and I will do my very best to sort them out.'

Emma believed her and knew that Miss Plath was the *only* teacher she had met at Blankton so far that she could really talk to. 'There must be others,' she thought, 'but I haven't met them.'

She put up her hand. 'Please, Miss Plath,' she said, 'have our sisters been told? Or do we have to tell them?'

'I'm glad you asked that, Emma. Your sisters will be told tomorrow by their class teacher,' she replied. 'But, we thought, if you knew today, you could talk to them tonight and prepare them for it. Do you agree?'

They all nodded. Emma knew it would be good for Fran, but whether *she* was going to have the courage to break more disturbing news tonight, after the problems of yesterday, she was not sure.

Chapter Fifteen

SITTING ON THE DOORSTEP—NOT ALLOWED

As THE last bell rang and they all got ready to go off to their billets, Emma's heart sank.

'How awful,' she thought, 'to go back to the Cricks' — another meal, another evening in that *awful* house.' It looked beautiful — spotlessly clean and tidy — not a bit like *their* house, where there were toys, books, papers, shoes and coats all over the place, despite Mum's attempts to persuade them to put things away. But Emma knew that their house was a *home*, a *real* home, not just a house that people lived in.

She went off to meet the others and saw Fran standing with Mary.

'Oh dear,' she thought. 'I've got to tell her that she's only got one more day here — then another school.'

But Fran was talking excitedly to Mary.

'Can we go and get them now?' she was asking.

'Get what?' enquired Emma.

'The broken biscuits of course,' said Fran.

With everything else that was happening, Emma had forgotten about the trip to the biscuit factory.

'That'll mean we don't get back to the Cricks quite so soon,' she said.

'*And* we'll have something extra to eat,' said Fran. 'Don't like going to bed hungry.'

They joined Pat, Annie and Benjie at the front of the school and went off in the opposite direction to the gypsy alley, chatting about the day's activities as they went. Emma was rather quiet. She did not feel quite as jolly as the others sounded — including Fran.

Then, a happy thought struck her — 'Bill.'

'Fran,' she said excitedly, 'we're going to see Bill on Saturday.'

'How can we?' asked Fran. The others stopped to listen.

'Marvellous,' said Pat.

'You won't half be glad to see your brother,' said Mary. 'Hope he's got a nice billet.'

'We'll soon find out,' said Emma.

'One more whole day, then it's Saturday,' said Fran happily.

'Two more nights in the Crick's house,' said Emma glumly. 'But at least we'll be able to tell Bill all about it.'

By this time, they had reached the enormous brick building of the biscuit factory.

'Come on, round the side,' said Pat and they followed her through a side gate into a little shed with a notice on the door —

BROKEN BISCUITS
½d a bag.

She went up to the counter, handed over her halfpenny and returned to them with a big bag of broken biscuits.

'One piece each,' she said. 'Take your pick.'

All kinds of biscuit pieces were mixed together in that bag. They made up their minds and each took a piece. Pat closed the bag and handed it to Emma.

'Hide this in your school bag and you can eat bits in your room before you go to bed,' she said.

'Be like a midnight feast,' laughed Annie.

'Better not be midnight,' joined in Mary, 'otherwise you'll have Madam Crick after you — and make sure you don't drop any crumbs.'

'I'll say,' said Emma, 'We don't want to leave her any clues.'

Finally, they reached the church hall and waved goodbye to each other.

'See you tomorrow,' called Pat, as they walked off.

Emma suddenly remembered there was something she needed to know.

'Stay there, Fran,' she said and ran after Pat.

Panting, she said, 'Do you know where Wood Lane Church of England School is?'

'That's it,' said Pat, 'behind the church hall. Why?'

'Well, Fran's got to go there from Monday,' Emma replied quietly. 'She's not allowed to stay at Blankton.' Lowering her voice even more, she continued, 'I've got to tell her tonight.'

'You poor things,' said Mary, looking upset. 'After yesterday — now this. Flippin' evacuation.'

'Look,' said Pat, 'tell Fran that on Saturday, at the evacuees' party, I'll introduce her to some of the boys and girls who go to Wood Lane. Then at least she'll *know* some of them and can start making friends.'

'Good,' said Mary. 'It won't be as scary for her if she knows them — and they know her.'

'Thanks,' said Emma, feeling relieved — and glad she'd spoken to them.

'Emma,' called Fran, 'when are you coming?' She was obviously fed-up with waiting.

'Now,' said Emma and ran back to her.

They arrived at the Crick's house and rang the bell. No-one came. They rang again. *Still* no-one came.

'I think she's out,' said Emma, not sure whether to be pleased, or sorry.

'What shall we do?' asked Fran, looking upset.

'I don't think there's much we *can* do,' replied Emma, ''cept wait.'

'Where?' asked Fran.

'Let's sit on the doorstep,' said Emma. 'We can't just walk up and down the road.'

They sat on the step, which was a bit cold, but, being Mrs Crick's step, it was *perfectly* clean.

'Can we have a nibble of biscuit?' asked Fran. 'I'm starving.'

'Can't see why not,' said Emma. She opened her school bag *and* the paper bag, without taking it out. 'Then if Madam Crick suddenly appears, she won't see it,' she explained.

Fran put her hand in the bag and pulled out half a chocolate biscuit.

'Yummy,' she said.

Emma put *her* hand in the bag and brought out a small piece of plain biscuit. Feeling glad it was that way round, she thought it was a good time to tell Fran the next piece of news.

'Miss Plath was talking to some of us today,' she said, as casually as she could, 'and explained that our younger sisters could not keep coming to Blankton — they'd have to go to another school.'

Fran's face dropped. Even the lovely taste of the chocolate biscuit could not prevent her from being upset about *another* change in arrangements.

'But why?' she asked tearfully. 'I *like* it in Blankton Prep.'

'I know, Fran,' said Emma sympathetically, 'but girls at Blankton either have to win a scholarship, or pay fees.'

'What are fees?' asked Fran.

'Well,' replied Emma, 'your Mum and Dad have to pay money for you to go there — not like an ordinary school.'

'Is it *lots* of money?' asked Fran.

' 'Fraid so,' said Emma. 'Mum and Dad haven't got lots of money.'

'Yep,' agreed Fran. 'Mum's purse is usually empty when she comes home with the week's shopping. So what's going to happen to me?'

'You're going to that nice school by the church hall,' replied Emma.

'How do you *know* it's a nice school?' asked Fran, still looking troubled.

'That's what I was talking to Pat about, just now,' replied Emma. 'She knows a lot of the children who go to Wood Lane and, at the evacuees' party on Saturday, she's going to introduce you to some of them.'

'So at least I'll know *somebody*,' said Fran, pathetically.

'Yes,' said Emma, 'and you'll know the young sisters who've been at Blankton Prep with you. They'll all be coming.'

'That's all right then,' said Fran. 'They're nice. But one thing, I'll *never* come back here alone. I'll be too scared.'

'Don't worry,' Emma reassured her. 'You can either wait for me by the church hall, or start walking to meet me.'

'Goody,' said Fran, smiling. 'I'll go and spy on the gypsies — and smell the lovely smells from their pot.'

'Be careful,' warned Emma. 'Those gypsy boys are rascals. They'll enjoy teasing you.'

Fran giggled. 'I shall *like* getting to know them,' she said.

'*What* are you doing, sitting on my nice clean step,' a familiar voice rang out. 'Get up — *at once*.'

They speedily jumped up, as Mrs Crick pushed Shirley in her pushchair up the path.

'Don't let me *ever* see you doing that again,' she said.

'What a greeting!' thought Emma. 'She didn't even say 'Hello' before she started — let alone apologise for keeping us locked out.'

Mrs Crick opened the front door. She lifted Shirley out of the pushchair. Emma and Fran stood and waited, not sure about going in. Next, Mrs Crick carried the pushchair into the hall and stood it on a piece of clean newspaper.

'Come along,' she said to them, sharply. 'And take your shoes off.'

They did as they were told and carried their shoes into the kitchen, placing them by the back door.

'You will have your tea in about ten minutes. I'll give you a call,' said Mrs Crick — and *nothing* else.

'At least we know what she expects us to do,' thought Emma as they climbed the stairs.

'She didn't say she was sorry to be late home,' whispered Fran, when the bedroom door was shut.

'Nor what we are supposed to do if we're not allowed to sit on the step,' added Emma.

'Wonder what she expects us to do if it rains,' said Emma.

'Get wet!' laughed Emma. *'Then* we'll be in trouble over our messy clothes and shoes.'

'Wonder what she'll give us for tea today,' said Fran.

'More sandwiches, I expect,' replied Emma, gloomily.

'But she can't give us sandwiches *every* day,' burst out Fran.

'Bet she can — and will,' said Emma, pulling a face. 'Better wash our hands and tidy our hair, before she calls.'

Using the cold water, they washed their hands and made sure the wash basin was *very* clean, before they went back into the bedroom to comb their hair. Then they sat on the bed and waited.

Soon the call came and they carefully walked down the stairs, along the hall carpet and into the kitchen. What did they see on the table? A small plate of sandwiches and two cups of weak tea.

Emma did not dare to look at Fran as she sat down.

'I will go and bath Shirley, whilst you have your tea,' said Mrs Crick, exactly as she had done last night.

120

'Please, can I just tell you about Saturday?' asked Emma nervously.

'What about Saturday?' Mrs Crick was *very* abrupt.

'Well, in the morning, we're going to school to see our brother,' replied Emma, feeling her legs and fingers twitching. 'In the afternoon there's a party at the church hall.'

'What about dinner? Are you having that at school?' Mrs Crick demanded to know.

'Well — no,' stammered Emma. 'I–I don't think so.'

'My sister and her husband are coming to dinner on Saturday so you won't be able to eat with us. I'll leave something out for you in the kitchen,' Mrs Crick told them in her usual hard-hearted way. 'What about Sunday?'

'Well — nothing's happening on Sunday,' said Emma nervously. 'We'll–we'll be here.'

'Well *we won't*,' said Mrs Crick. 'We always go to my mother's on Sunday, so I'll leave you something on the kitchen table.'

She picked up Shirley and started going out of the door. 'When you've finished your tea, put the things on the draining board,' she said. 'I'll call you in the morning.' And that was it! She had gone without a single friendly word — and lots of unfriendly ones.

'I don't think she likes us,' moaned Fran.

'Don't think it's just us — I think it would have been the same for any evacuees she was told to have,' said Emma, feeling just as miserable tonight as she had last night.

'Better tonight,' whispered Fran. 'We *are* going to have some more to eat — upstairs in the bedroom!'

Emma giggled and felt better.

Chapter Sixteen

REUNION WITH BILL

AT LAST Saturday came and Emma and Fran set off for school.

'Funny, going to school on a Saturday,' said Fran, as they walked past the gypsy camp.

'Better than staying in that house with Madam Crick,' returned Emma.

' 'ello,' said a little voice and a face appeared out from behind a tree.

The girls stopped.

'Hello,' said Emma. 'What's your name?'

'Nellie,' said the little gypsy girl, 'like my Mum. Will you play with me?'

'Sorry, said Emma gently. 'We've got to go to school. P'raps we'll see you on the way back.'

'Come 'ere, Nellie,' called her mother. 'Don't you bother them young ladies.'

'She's not bothering us,' called Emma. 'We're just making friends.'

The gypsy's face broke into a smile.

'Nice,' she said. 'All the other kids is boys. She ain't got no girls to play wiv.'

'We're going to school now,' said Emma. 'We'll call out to her on the way back. 'Bye. 'Bye, Nellie.'

The little girl waved, a disappointed look on her face.

'Bless you,' called Nellie's mother. 'She'll be pleased.'

As they continued walking along the path, Fran said, 'Weren't they nice?'

'Think I'd rather live with the gypsies in the caravans than with Madam Crick,' replied Emma, with a great deal of feeling.

They hurried along to the school, excited about seeing Bill.

'There he is,' cried Fran. 'There he is!' She rushed into the playground with Emma running behind.

'Bill,' she called. 'Bill.' He turned round and saw them, left his group of friends and hurried over with a big grin on his face.

'Great,' he said. 'It's great to see you. Where are you staying? How are you getting on?'

They told him their sad story and he listened very sympathetically.

'You poor things,' he said. 'That's terrible. I wish I knew what we could do about it. P'raps when Mum comes she'll be able to make them find you somewhere nice.'

'Where is Mum? When is she coming?' asked Emma excitedly.

'She's in a little village near Reading, but now she knows we're here, she's going to move into the town,' Bill explained.

'How do you know all this?' asked a surprised Emma. 'Have you heard from Dad?'

'Well, it's luck really,' replied Bill. 'I'm staying with some really lovely ladies, the Misses Noble, and their Dad. Their other sister came to see them two days ago and was still there when I got home from school, so I had tea with them.'

'You did what?' exploded the astounded Emma. 'Madam Crick's sister is coming to dinner today, so *we* have to eat in the kitchen — can't have it with them.'

Bill went on. 'She was talking about evacuees — a mother and her young son.'

'Jonty?' asked Emma breathlessly.

'Yes,' grinned Bill, 'Jonty.'

Fran was jumping up and down with excitement clapping her hands.

'Goody good,' she said. 'We know where they are. When can we see them?'

'Not sure yet,' said Bill, 'but Miss Noble's trying to find a billet for them in our road.'

'In *your* road,' said Emma enviously. 'Lucky thing. Do you think she'll be able to?'

'Sure she will,' said Bill. 'They've got lots of friends. Everyone seems to like the Nobles.'

'Wish they could find somewhere for us,' said Fran, miserably.

''Fraid it's too far away from your school,' said Bill. 'We're on the other side of Reading. It'd be a long way to go every morning — and bus fares cost a lot.'

Emma would not let herself think about miserable things at the moment. The thought of seeing Mum again and being able to pour out all their troubles, cheered her up enormously.

'What are you doing tomorrow?' asked Bill.

'Nothing,' replied Emma. '*She's* going to her mother for the day, so we'll be alone at the Crick's.'

'She's going to leave us there with food in the kitchen,' said Fran gloomily.

'Funny old Sunday that will be,' went on Emma, thinking of Sunday dinners at home, when plates were piled high with vegetables from the allotment and the table was crowded because Dad had invited one or two soldiers, or airmen to join them.

'No you won't be sitting there alone,' said Bill, with a grin. 'The Misses Noble have said, if you don't mind a long walk, you can come round and have dinner with us!'

'*Can* we?' Emma's eyes nearly popped out of her head.

'Coo,' said Fran, 'thought we were just going to have rotten old sandwiches again.'

125

'How will we know where to find you?' asked Emma.

'I'll meet you outside this school at about eleven,' replied Bill. 'Then we can walk back together.'

'How will you know where to find this school on your own?' Emma asked.

'I won't be on my own,' said Bill. 'There's a boy next door, about my age, and he's said he'll come with me.'

'Aren't some people kind,' said Emma. 'Wish we could have stayed with Phil. She and Charlie were like that.'

'I'm sorry,' said Bill — and sounded as if he really meant it. 'P'raps it won't be for long. P'raps there won't be an invasion and we'll be able to go home.'

'I forgot that's what it was all about,' laughed Emma. 'I was so worried about what was happening to *us*, that I forgot why we'd been sent here!'

'Don't you hear the wireless, or see the newspapers?' asked Bill in a surprised voice.

'Oh no,' said Emma, 'we're just bundled upstairs. We haven't been into any other downstairs room, except the kitchen, so I don't know whether they've got a wireless. Or take a newspaper.'

'What happened when you were with your lovely Phil then?' Bill wanted to know.

'We were doing exciting things, like going in the back of Charlie's car to buy fish and chips for supper,' Emma told him.

'Lucky things,' said Bill.

'We *would* have been, if it had lasted,' retorted Emma.

'Sorry,' muttered Bill.

'Hi,' called a girl's voice.

Emma turned. It was Audrey coming over to them with a boy who looked just like her — except for the hair.

'The boys know each other,' said Audrey 'and I know

126

Emma and Fran. We came together on the train.'

They stood chatting happily together until a whistle blew.

'The reunion is over for now,' said a Blankton master. 'I promise that we will arrange another in a few weeks. However, because you have now met and been able to exchange information, you may be able to plan regular meetings between yourselves.

'One last thing I would like to say. If you are worried about what is happening in Kent because you have not heard from your parents and you have not been able to listen to the wireless — *nothing* has changed. *Nothing* has changed.'

A boy's hand shot up. 'When can we go home, sir?' he asked.

'Listen, young Bobby,' said the master, 'you've only just arrived. You can't expect to go back *so* soon. Enjoy the broken biscuits. Don't have those in *our* city.'

'Broken biscuits?' 'Broken biscuits?' The murmur went round.

Emma and Fran giggled. They had a bag of broken biscuits in their room and had enjoyed them for two nights.

'See you tomorrow then,' said Bill, as he and Audrey's brother went off with the other boys.

'Lovely,' said Emma.

' 'Bye,' said Fran.

'Lucky things,' said Audrey when the two boys had gone.

'His hostesses have invited us to Sunday dinner,' explained Emma.

'That's nice of them,' said Audrey.

'Would have been a bit miserable if they hadn't,' said

Emma and told Audrey about Madam Crick and how awful it was living there.

Audrey was full of sympathy as they walked off together.

At the entrance to the path between the trees and the fields, they parted company.

'I go up here,' said Audrey.

'And we've promised to play with a little gypsy girl,' said Emma.

'Mind you're not late home for your dragon,' Audrey reminded them. 'She's likely to throw your dinner in the ash bin if you're not there to eat it.'

Emma chuckled and Fran giggled. 'It's good to be able to laugh about horrible things,' thought Emma.

Nellie was waiting for them as they approached the gypsy camp.

'You must have been waiting here a long time,' said Emma and Nellie nodded.

'Will you play with me now?' she asked.

'Yes we will,' said Fran.

'For a little while,' said Emma. 'What shall we play?'

'Stories,' said the little girl. 'I like stories. Tell me some.'

This surprised Emma, but she knew it was something she could cope with.

'Come on then,' she said. 'Let's sit under this tree.'

'Which story shall we have?' Emma asked Nellie.

'What about Goldilocks?' suggested Fran. 'Then we can all join in.'

The next half an hour passed happily. Emma made the Father Bear voice, Fran was Mother Bear and Nellie was Baby Bear. She loved it.

'Will you come again?' she pleaded.

'Yes,' said Fran. 'I'll come and tell you stories every day

after school. Emma can meet me here.'

The faces of the two little girls beamed and Emma felt much happier about next week and the week after.

'Nellie, come on,' called her mother. 'Let the young ladies go now.'

'See you again on Monday,' said Fran to Nellie.

'Bless you,' said the gypsy lady with a big smile.

' 'Bye, Nellie,' called the girls as they walked off up the path.

Nellie stood waving until they reached the corner.

Chapter Seventeen

MADAM CRICK SULKS

EMMA knocked on the door of 34, dreading the reception they would get. Her spirits lifted when *Mr* Crick answered.

'Come in,' he said in a kind voice. 'Had a good morning?'

'Yes,' smiled Emma, as she knelt down to take her shoes off. 'We saw our brother.'

'I'm very glad,' said Mr Crick. 'You must feel happier now you've linked up with some of your family again.'

'Come along Albert,' shouted Madam Crick from the dining room. 'Give the girls their dinner in the kitchen and come back here. *Don't* stand there talking.'

'No dear,' Mr Crick called back, as they followed him into the kitchen. He closed the door very gently behind him. 'Sorry about that,' he whispered. 'I've tried to keep your dinner hot, but I'm not sure whether I've managed.'

He pulled two plates of food out of the oven — sausage meat, a few peas and one potato on each.

'Hope that's enough,' he said doubtfully, as he put the plates on the table.

'Come *along*, Albert,' the voice shouted again.

''Bye,' he said and went quickly out of the kitchen.

'Poor man,' whispered Emma. 'He's nice — but scared of her.'

'Let's eat,' said Fran and took a mouthful. 'It's cold — good job I like cold sausage meat! But I don't like cold spuds and peas.'

'Wonder what they've had to eat in the dining room?' whispered Emma. They were soon to know.

Mrs Crick and her sister pushed open the kitchen door carrying dirty plates and dishes. The remains of peas, carrots, roast potatoes *and* boiled potatoes were in the dishes and traces of gravy could be seen on the plates.

'Hurry up girls,' said Mrs Crick. 'We shall be needing the table to put things on.'

'Yes, Mrs Crick,' said Emma, hastily swallowing what was in her mouth. She watched, wide-eyed, whilst a beautifully decorated trifle was taken from the larder and carried out of the kitchen by the sister.

'When you've finished,' said Madam, 'put your plates on the draining board and go upstairs until you're ready to go out.'

'Yes, Mrs Crick,' said Emma. 'Just one thing — tomorrow, we're going out to Sunday dinner, so you don't have to leave us anything.'

'Good,' said Madam, as she left the kitchen to follow her sister back ionto the dining room.

'She didn't even ask where we are going,' Emma hissed to Fran.

'She's horrid — really horrid,' Fran's voice trembled as she spoke. 'Emma, *how* long do we have to stay here?'

'I don't know,' said Emma mournfully. 'Every day is a day too long.'

'Do you think we're going to get any trifle?' whispered Fran.

'Don't think so,' Emma whispered back. 'She just said — eat up and get out!'

They quickly finished off the sausage meat, struggled with the cold potatoes and peas, put their plates on the draining board and went upstairs. Closing the bedroom door, Emma plonked down on the bed.

'Thank goodness we're going to that party this afternoon,' she said.

'And we're going to see Bill tomorrow,' added Fran. 'Wouldn't it have been awful if we'd had nothing to do?'

'Let's play Snakes and Ladders,' said Emma. 'Then we'll leave early to go to that party.'

They played, not caring who won, just passing the time. Voices and the clatter of plates could be heard downstairs.

'Wonder if there was any trifle left,' said Emma.

'Not for *us*,' laughed Emma. 'Come on. Let's get ready and go.'

They washed, combed their hair and crept downstairs to collect their shoes from the kitchen. Fortunately, no-one was around. From the sound of cups and saucers in the dining room, it seemed as if they were drinking tea.

'Quick let's get out.' Emma said to Fran, who was eying half a dish of trifle on the kitchen table.

'Don't you *dare* touch it,' she warned Fran, in a whisper. 'Madam'll kill us if you do.' They crept out of the kitchen to the front door.

' 'Bye,' they called out, as they opened it.

Mr Crick appeared. 'Are you off girls?' he asked. 'What time do you think you'll be back?'

'We don't know,' said Emma.

'Don't worry,' he said. 'We'll be here to let you in.'

'Albert,' the voice called. 'Come back in here. Let them

go.' He returned to the dining room and, thankfully, they left the house.

Slowly they walked to the church hall, knowing that they were very early. But, it did not matter. Anything was better than that house.

The afternoon and early evening passed happily. Pat introduced them to a lot of people, grown-ups and children. Everyone was very friendly and they had a lovely tea. Emma noticed that there was a strange silence when she told grown-ups that they were staying with the Cricks, in answer to questions.

'Does *everyone* know how horrid she is?' she wondered.

Finally it was time to walk back. Fran was chatting happily. 'That school'll be O.K.,' she said. 'I've met lots of nice children and two of the teachers.'

Emma felt relieved that something was going right.

Mr Crick opened the door again for them. Shirley was in his arms and there were no voices coming from the living room.

'Had a good party?' he asked in a very quiet voice.

'Oh yes,' he went on, still very quietly. 'Will half past eight be all right for breakfast tomorrow?'

'Fine,' said Emma. 'We're meeting our brother at the High School and then going back to dinner with him.'

'That's lovely,' said Mr Crick, looking relieved.

'Goodnight,' said Emma, as they began to climb the stairs. 'Night,' she said to Shirley and gave a little wave. Shirley smiled.

At the top of the stairs, Emma looked along the landing. Outside the Crick's bedroom was a tray. On it, were a few sandwiches, a cake, a small pot of tea, milk, and a cup and saucer.

'That's odd,' she whispered to Fran, as they went into their room. Shortly afterwards, they heard Mr Crick

133

climbing the stairs and tapping on the bedroom door.

Emma listened hard and she heard him say quietly, 'Your tea's out here. Unlock the door and let me hand it in.'

'No,' shouted Madam Crick. 'Take it away. I don't want it.'

Without saying another word, Mr Crick went down the stairs.

'Get's odder,' whispered Emma.

'Has she locked herself in her bedroom?' asked Fran in a shocked voice.

'Seems so,' replied Emma.

'Funny lady,' said Fran. 'Let's get ready for bed.'

'Then we'll play noughts and crosses until we drop off to sleep,' said Emma. 'P'raps the morning will come quickly, so that we can get out of this house again and go somewhere where people are happy.'

As Emma finally fell asleep that night, she wondered, 'Where's *he* going to sleep, if *she* won't unlock the door?'

In the morning when they got up and used the bathroom, the house was strangely quiet. At half past eight they went downstairs and waited in the kitchen. They waited — and waited. Finally, Mr Crick appeared with Shirley in his arms.

'Sorry to be late,' he said, looking upset. 'I didn't sleep very well — and then, I overslept. Shirley didn't wake me up for a change.'

Emma did not ask him where he had slept, as he bustled around getting out dishes, cereal, milk and sugar. Then he put the kettle on and she said, 'Don't worry we've got plenty of time.'

They ate their cereal and he made the tea. He poured out mugs of tea for the girls and two cups.

'I'll leave Shirley here with you for a minute,' he said, taking one of the cups and saucers out of the kitchen.

Shirley seemed very happy to stay with Emma and Fran. She toddled across to where they were sitting, unaware that upstairs, her father was knocking on a locked bedroom door and her mother was shouting at him. A few minutes later, Mr Crick returned with the cup of tea still in his hand. Without a word, he tipped it down the sink and sat at the table to silently drink his own.

Emma felt very embarrassed, so to hide that, she played with Shirley. Fran and the little girl laughed. Mr Crick gave a relieved smile.

'Thanks,' he said. 'What time will you be back?'

'We don't know,' said Emma.

'Look,' he said, 'I'm not sure what's going to happen to us

today, so I'll give you a door key. Whatever time you come back, you'll be able to let yourselves in.'

He fished in a little jar on the dresser and handed Emma a key.

'Just one thing,' he added, 'you'd better knock first, in case we're here. Hang on to the key all the time you're living here. You might need it.'

'Thank you very much,' said Emma, feeling happier. 'At least we won't be sitting on the doorstep again,' she thought.

'Shall we wash up?' she asked.

'No that's all right,' said Mr Crick. 'You just get ready and go.'

'Thanks,' said Emma and Fran, as they scurried away up the stairs to get ready. Emma knew that she wanted to get out of the house before Madam Crick appeared — and she had a feeling that that's what Mr Crick wanted too.

In no time at all, they were going out of the front door, waving goodbye to him and Shirley.

Chapter Eighteen

JUST LIKE HOME

THEY arrived at the High School early and knew that they had a long wait for Bill, but did not mind. Perching on a brick wall that had its railings removed for the 'war effort,' they watched people going to church.

A Salvation Army Band marched by, with soldiers and airmen playing cornets, trombones and euphoniums, amongst the uniformed Salvationists.

'Must be nice to belong to something like that, if you're away from home,' said Emma as they sat, enjoying the music.

'Well, Bill plays the trombone and Jimmy Turner the cornet,' said Fran. 'Can't they join?'

'No, silly — they belong to the *City* Band, that's different,' Emma told her.

'Sounds the same,' said Fran.

As the band marched off into the distance, Fran asked, 'Why *did* they take all these iron railings and things away?' She was pushing her fingers into the holes left behind in the wall as she spoke.

'To make guns and tanks,' replied Emma.

'How can you make guns with bits of fence?' Fran was still puzzled.

'They melt it all down and start again,' Emma told her.

'But iron's jolly hard,' said Fran.

'And the fires that do the melting are jolly hot,' laughed Emma. She was glad to see Bill and another boy turning the corner, because she knew she couldn't answer any more questions about how iron fences could be turned into guns and tanks — she really did not know!

Fran jumped off the wall and ran towards the boys. Emma followed.

'Hi,' said Bill. 'These are my sisters, Emma and Fran,' he told the other boy. 'This is Cecil,' he told the girls.

'Hello,' they said shyly.

'Quite a long walk to the Nobles,' said Bill.

'We won't mind,' replied Emma. 'Better than being with the Cricks.' She went on to tell him the latest in the saga.

'Locked herself in the bedroom!' Bill was amazed.

'Bit like a naughty kid,' added Cecil, 'not a grown-up.'

They chatted as they walked and really did not notice how far it was. At last they turned into a road of neat terraced houses, with net curtains — and polished doorsteps.

'Here we are. Our road,' said Bill and he led the way up to a front door.

' 'Bye,' said Cecil. 'See you later.' He went into his own house.

'His Dad's in the Navy,' Bill told them, as he knocked the door. 'He gets a bit fed up sometimes — misses him.'

The door opened and a plump, friendly lady wearing a pinafore over her dress, greeted them with a warm smile.

'Hel-lo,' she said. 'I'm so pleased to meet you, Emma and Fran. Bill's told us so much about you.'

Another lady appeared. She was smaller, but her face was just as friendly.

'Come in, come in, my dears,' she said and they all walked into the hall.

'Dad's in the front room reading the paper. At least, that's what he says he's doing,' she laughed. 'I think he's been peeping out through the curtains looking for you!'

She opened the front room door. Emma hesitated and asked, 'Shall we take our shoes off?'

'Shall you *what*?' asked the first lady looking surprised.

Emma stumbled over her words. 'Madam–Mrs–our hostess–makes us take our shoes off as soon as we go through the door,' she explained.

'Have you got slippers to put on then?' the lady asked. 'Well no, we didn't bring any, so we just go around in our socks,' replied Emma.

'How stupid,' said the second lady. 'We don't do things like that here. Come and meet Dad.'

Mr Noble was sitting in an armchair by the window in his shirt sleeves, a pullover and his best trousers. He stood up as they came in.

'Come on in girls,' he said. 'Aren't I lucky 'avin' all you young 'uns around.'

He held out his hand and shook theirs warmly.

'You all sit and talk to Dad whilst we finish getting the dinner ready,' said the plump Miss Noble.

'I'm sure he'll find lots of stories to tell you,' laughed the other Miss Noble and they both bustled off.

'Sit down,' said Mr Noble — he pulled up some smaller armchairs for Emma and Bill and a little foot stool for Fran.

They laughed about lots of things. He told them stories about old Reading and the biscuit factory. They told him

139

about Kenabury and the planes fighting overhead all through the summer.

He picked up his Sunday paper again and pointed to the front page.

'They haven't invaded yet,' he said, 'and our boys seem to be winning the Battle of Britain.'

'Will the war be over soon?' asked Bill eagerly.

'Well, no,' said Mr Noble sadly. 'They may not manage to invade us, but they're still in all those other countries, like France, Holland and Belgium. We've got to get them out!'

'*We* have?' asked Emma anxiously. 'On our own?'

'How *can* we?' Bill did not look too happy. 'It could take years.'

'I'm afraid it could,' agreed the old man. 'Just like it did in the First World War. They've come from the colonies to help.'

'What's the colonies?' asked Fran, puzzled.

'Well,' said Mr Noble looking down at her and putting his hand gently on her shoulder. 'It's all those other countries that share our King — like Canada, India, Australia and New Zealand.'

'Not America?' asked Emma.

'No, not America,' laughed Mr Noble. 'They left us a long time ago, but *might* come and help — one day.'

'Dinner,' called the smaller Miss Noble, poking her head round the door.

The old man got up from his chair and, as they went into the living room, the lovely smells of Sunday dinner greeted them.

'Sit down all of you,' said the plump Miss Noble. 'Girls on this side and Bill opposite.'

When they were all seated, dishes of steaming vegetables,

roast potatoes and meat with Yorkshire pudding, were carried in.

'Just like home on Sunday,' thought Emma.

'Not much meat,' laughed the old man, 'but plenty of vegetables.'

'That's what Dad says,' chukled Emma, 'when we have soldiers and airmen to Sunday dinner!'

'Dad grows lots of vegetables on the allotment,' said the plump Miss Noble.

'We help him,' the other Miss Noble added.

'Like us,' said Bill. 'Dad's out there all his spare time, then we go and help picking peas and things.'

'Now before we start, let's say Grace,' said Miss Noble gently. They all closed their eyes and repeated.

'For what we are about to receive,

May the Lord make us truly thankful. Amen.'

'Amen,' repeated Mr Noble. 'Now come on. Help yourselves. Don't be afraid to eat.'

'Makes a change to hear that again,' thought Emma.

'We'll lift the dishes,' said the plump Miss Noble and between the two of them, the plates were soon piled high with lovely food. The small pieces of meat were hidden under roast potatoes and crispy Yorkshire pudding.

'Now Winnie,' said the old man to the plump Miss Noble. 'You've got some good news for them, haven't you?'

She smiled broadly. 'Yes,' she said. 'This morning I went along the road to see a friend of mine. She's a widow. Lives in the house all by herself and gets a bit lonely. I talked to her about your Mum and Jonty.'

She paused. All eyes were on her — waiting to hear the next bit of news.

'She'll have them!' Miss Winnie exclaimed.

'Great,' shouted Bill.

'Goody good,' said Emma.

'That's mar–vell–ous,' breathed Emma, unable at first to believe their good luck.

'When can they come?' asked Bill.

'Our sister's coming across this afternoon — bringing someone with her,' said Miss Winnie with a little grin.

'You mean — Mum?' Emma could hardly believe what she was hearing. 'Mum's coming?'

'Here — today?' echoed Bill and Fran. They were all so excited by the news that they stopped eating.

'Eat up,' laughed the old man. 'Don't let it get cold. Give them some more roast potatoes, Millie,' he told his other daughter.

Miss Millie lifted the dish and gave them another one each.

'I nearly didn't tell you — and let your Mum's visit be a complete surprise,' said Miss Winnie. 'We arranged it the other day when our sister was here. But now that we've

fixed a billet up the road, there'll be lots to organise and Mrs Smith would like to meet your Mum.'

Emma, Fran and Bill were so thrilled that they could *still* hardly eat.

'Should have waited 'til after dinner to tell them,' said Miss Millie.

'Couldn't keep it a secret any longer,' said the old man. 'I know what it's like to be away from your family. *Hated* that in the First World War.'

'This dinner's lovely,' said Emma, really enjoying it.

'Mm,' agreed Fran. 'Won't want any broken biscuits in bed tonight.'

'Any what?' asked Miss Winnie with a laugh.

'Well,' explained Emma. 'Since we've been at the Cricks, we've been so hungry, that one of our friends bought us some broken biscuits from the factory. We keep them hidden in our room and eat them in bed.'

'You poor little girls,' said Miss Millie, looking very unhappy.

'You'd better come to Sunday dinner every week,' said Miss Winnie.

'That would be love–ly,' said Fran, with a big sigh of relief. Emma and Bill laughed.

'If it's not too much trouble for you,' said Emma, 'it would be jolly nice for us. I was *dreading* Sundays at the Cricks.'

'That's it then,' said old Mr Noble. 'Be a real treat for me too.'

A large home-made apple pie, with custard, followed the roast dinner and Emma felt pretty full as she left the table.

'Can I help wash up?' she asked, anxious to make a small contribution to this lovely Sunday.

'Would you like to?' asked Miss Millie.

'I'd love to,' said Emma. 'It feels like home to be helping. Mrs Crick just wants us out of the kitchen and into the bedroom. She doesn't trust us with washing up things. 'Spect she thinks we'll break something.'

'If you want to,' laughed Miss Winnie, 'You can help prepare tea too.'

'Great,' said Emma and followed them into the kitchen.

'We'll retire to the front room and go on talking,' said Mr Noble to Fran and Bill.

Chapter Nineteen

MUM AND JONTY ARRIVE!

'THEY'RE here. They're here.' Emma heard Fran shouting excitedly. Everyone crowded into the hall as the bell rang.

'Open the door, Bill,' said Miss Winnie. He did — and there were Mum and Jonty!

Emma was so happy, she was crying — relieved to be seeing Mum again, just when she needed her most. After huge hugs and kisses, they all went into the front room and the Nobles disappeared.

'We'll go and make you a cup of tea,' said Miss Millie.

'How nice,' thought Emma. 'They're leaving us alone to talk and catch up.'

And catch up they did, all trying to get a word in — so much seemed to have happened since they got onto those trains at the West Station.

Mum was very upset to hear about the girls change of billet. She did not like the sound of Mrs Crick one little bit. What could she do? She, like Emma, felt trapped and helpless. But, she was sure of one thing — they would all go home as soon as it was safe.

She said to them, 'I've been reading the papers and

listening to the wireless. There may not be an invasion. All of that fighting in the sky by our airmen, might have saved us. In a few weeks, we'll know — and as soon as we can, we'll all go home.'

They all breathed a sigh of relief. 'We won't be evacuees for any longer than we need to be,' she told them.

'I'm lucky,' said Bill. 'The Nobles are great.'

'Yes,' agreed Mum. 'Jonty and I are lucky too — and are going to be even luckier thanks to the Nobles. But, we can't let Emma and Fran go on living with that awful woman.'

'Anyway,' said Bill. 'I'll bet Dad's lonely without us.'

'Oh he is,' said Mum.

'How do you know?' asked the astounded Emma.

'Well, I suddenly remembered that Dad's boss has a phone — and I had the number in my little book,' Mum replied. 'So, the other night, Bert, that's my host, came with me to the phone box and he rang the number for me.

When he passed the phone to me, I felt pretty nervous. That's the first time I've used the phone.'

'Then what happened?' asked Bill. They could hardly wait to hear.

'Well, Dad's boss was very kind and said if I rang again on Friday at six o'clock, he'd make sure Dad was there to speak to me!' said Mum triumphantly.

'Was he?' asked Emma.

'Yes,' Mum told them. 'He was just as thrilled as I was. I told him I knew I was seeing Bill today — of course, I didn't know about you girls.'

'He doesn't know we've moved?' commented Emma.

'He hasn't had cards from any of us, so until I phoned, he had no idea where we were,' said Mum.

'Bet he was relieved to have news of *some* of us,' said Bill.

'What next?' asked Emma.

'Well, my money ran out — it's very expensive to talk on the phone. He's going to phone me back to that phone box next Tuesday — I gave him the number,' said Mum. 'He *did* say that nothing had changed — the fighting in the air is still going on, there are more troops in the city — and it's *awful* with no children around.'

They heard the rattle of tea cups in the hall.

'Can we come in?' called Miss Winnie.

'Please do,' said Mum. 'Open the door, Bill.'

Soon they were all sitting round drinking tea and eating biscuits — *not* broken ones.

'Have you told Mum about our neighbour?' asked Miss Winnie.

'No,' said Bill. 'Thought it would be better if you did that.'

'He didn't say,' thought Emma, 'because we've had so much else to talk about that we didn't get round to it.'

147

The rest of the afternoon was spent in making lovely plans for Mum and Jonty to move in with Mrs Smith. Emma felt quite envious of the happiness she knew would be Bill's when Mum was living up the road.

'Mum and the Nobles too!' she thought. It didn't seem quite fair and when she met Mrs Smith, she knew that another nice person had come into their lives.

'Why do *we* have to suffer Madam Crick?'

She looked at the clock. Time was running out. They would soon have to begin the long walk back. It was not the walk that bothered her, but what they would find at the end of it.

Miss Millie's voice jolted her out of her unhappy thoughts.

'Emma,' she said, 'I wondered if these old slippers of mine would be useful to you.' In her hand, she had a pair of blue slippers with fur round them. They didn't look old to Emma!

Before Emma could say anything, she went on, 'Did I hear you tell your Mum that you needed some gloves?' Miss Millie asked.

'Well — yes,' said a surprised Emma.

'Try these then,' said Miss Millie and handed her a pair of knitted gloves.

Emma was so thrilled she could hardly speak.

'Thank you — thank you,' she said. 'You're so kind.' As she bent down to try on the slippers, she caught a glimpse of Fran's face and felt guilty at her own good luck.

Miss Millie saw it too.

'Don't worry, Fran,' she said. 'I'm going to make some slippers and some gloves for you.' Fran's face lit up.

'They'll be ready next Sunday. Just come into the kitchen with me and let me measure your feet.'

Miss Millie took Fran's hand and, as they went out of the

door, Emma said, 'They're lovely. Thank you.'

Sunday tea with home-made scones, jam and cakes was the best *family* meal that Emma had had since they left home. Only Dad was missing. She could imagine him, sitting at home alone — poor Dad — perhaps he was even more unlucky than she was.

After tea there were thanks, goodbyes — and promises of seeing each other next Sunday. On that lovely thought, Emma, Fran, Bill and Cecil set off down the road back towards the Cricks. Emma's legs felt just as they had on that morning when they walked to the West Station. They did *not* want to go — but there was no choice.

'Cheer up, Em,' whispered Bill, 'Mum understands and she'll make sure that you get away from that horrible woman as soon as possible.'

Emma felt like crying again. She and Bill were usually arguing and scrapping. Now, when she needed it most, he was being really kind and understanding. Perhaps he was not such a bad brother after all!

All too soon they reached the High School and the boys waved goodbye to the girls until they had turned the corner.

'That was a love–ly day,' breathed Emma.

'Love–ly,' echoed Fran.

'Listen,' Emma went on, 'whatever happens now, and the rest of this week, however horrible it is, just keep remembering next Sunday. Fix it in your head — and we'll get through the other days somehow.'

She squeezed Fran's hand and thought how much worse it would have been if she'd been at the Cricks completely alone.

Their reluctant feet finally brought them to 34 The Gardens. Emma knocked the door. No-one came. She knocked again. Still there was silence.

'They're out,' breathed Fran.

'Yes. They're out,' agreed Emma. 'Thank goodness.' She took the key out of her pocket and opened the front door.

They stopped inside and thankfully climbed the stairs of the silent house — better no people, than the wrong people.

Chapter Twenty

MISSING — PRESUMED DROWNED

THE next week was busy. Fran started her new school, made lots of nice friends and enjoyed spending time after school with Nellie, the little gypsy girl. She told her stories and played games until Emma and the others arrived.

Miss Plath continued to be nice, Miss Pring unbearable, particularly in speech training and Madam Crick's suppers did not change from being one small plate of sandwiches and a glass of squash each. The bedroom felt the only safe place in the house and Mr Crick seemed to be even more afraid than before of speaking to Emma and Fran.

On Saturday afternoon, some of the Blankton girls and their sisters, met in the park for games and chats. This helped, but it was Sunday that Emma was longing for — seeing Mum, Jonty and Bill, hearing news of Dad and sharing lovely family meals with the Nobles.

At last, Sunday arrived and after a hasty breakfast prepared by Mr Crick, Emma and Fran went off to meet Bill and Cecil. They perched on the wall and waited, watching the people going to church, the Salvation Army Band marching by and various dogs out for a morning walk.

Bill arrived — but no Cecil.

'Didn't he want to come?' asked a disappointed Emma.

'It wasn't that,' said Bill. 'His Mum had a telegram from the War Office yesterday about his Dad. It said — MISSING PRESUMED DROWNED.'

'How awful,' said Emma.

'What does that mean?' asked Fran.

'Well,' said Bill gently. 'His Dad's a sailor and his boat must have been sunk, so they don't know where he is.'

'Poor Cecil,' said Fran, looking very sad. 'Fancy losing your Dad like that. Glad our Dad's a fireman, not a sailor.'

'His Mum must be *very* upset,' said Emma.

'She is. They all are,' Bill told them. 'But, they're trying to be brave. I think they're hoping that his Dad's been picked up by another boat.'

'I hope so,' said Emma fervently. 'I really hope so.'

They walked on in silence, trying to imagine what it must feel like to get one of those terrible telegrams about your Dad.

As they turned into the Noble's road, Emma suddenly panicked. 'What shall we say if we see Cecil?' she asked Bill.

'I don't know,' he replied helplessly. 'What can you say — just — "I'm sorry".'

'It's worse for him if other children stop talking to him, because they don't know what to say,' said Emma thoughtfully.

'That's what Mr Noble said,' Bill told her. ' "Try and talk to Cecil," ' he said. "That will help. Don't hide away from him." '

They reached the Noble's house and Emma glanced next door to Cecil's. All of the curtains were drawn — a sign that someone had died.

'The house will be gloomy inside,' she thought, 'with no light coming in.'

Bill knocked at the door and Miss Winnie came. Cecil was with her.

'Cecil's having dinner with us,' she said. 'His Granny and Grandad are with his Mum. We thought you'd like that.'

'Oh yes,' Emma smiled at him. 'I'm glad you wanted to come.'

He smiled back weakly. His face was pale and puffy, as if he'd been crying a lot.

The front door closed behind them and the children all went into the front room with Mr Noble.

'Thank goodness he's with us,' thought Emma, feeling relieved. 'He'll know what to talk about — he's a wise old man.'

When they were all seated around on chairs and stools,

153

Mr Noble produced a mouth organ from his pocket and started playing —

'On Richmond Hill.

There lives a lass . . .'

Emma began humming the tune, followed by Fran, then Bill, singing the words. Cecil slowly joined in as the mouth organ moved from tune to tune, Emma saw his face relax.

When Miss Winnie called them for dinner, they had not talked but felt much more comfortable with each other, through singing together.

'You lovely man, Mr Noble,' Emma thought, 'to help us all through something that could have been difficult.'

She sat next to Cecil at the dinner table and was able to help him to vegetables, clear away his plate when they'd all finished and pass him his pudding when the apple pie was served. She learned that it was by doing *ordinary* things with people who are very unhappy, that you can both cope. It is not always words that show you care.

After dinner, Mr Noble said to the two boys, 'Would you like me to teach you how to play the mouth organ?'

'Ye-es,' said Bill enthusiastically. 'I can play the trombone, but didn't bring it with me.'

'I've had a go on my uncle's saxophone,' said Cecil. 'I'd love to be able to play an instrument.'

'Let's start with the mouth organ,' said Mr Noble. 'I've got a couple of extra ones. Then, young Cecil, I used to play the sax. It's in the attic, somewhere. I'll get it out and you can have proper lessons. We'll even give Bill a go to save him missing his trombone too much.'

'Can I come and listen?' asked Fran eagerly.

'You don't mind boys, do you?' asked Mr Noble.

'Course not,' said Cecil.

'I'll help with the washing up,' said Emma.

'You don't have to,' Miss Millie told her.

'But I want to,' replied Emma.

When they were in the kitchen, surrounded by dirty plates, dishes, saucepans and tea towels, Emma asked, 'Is Mum coming down?'

'Yes,' said Miss Winnie, smiling, 'about half past two.'

'Oh good,' said Emma. 'I'll be so pleased to see her again.'

To the sounds of three mouth organs, one making tunes, the other two, not always hitting the right notes, the washing up started. Emma found herself talking about Mrs Crick and Miss Pring — all the nasty things.

Then she stopped. 'There are lots of nice people,' she said, blushing, afraid that they'd think she was a moaner.

'Get it off your chest girl,' said Miss Winnie. 'We don't mind listening.'

Washing up done — tea prepared — and the bell rang. The music stopped and they all ran to the front door. Cecil came into the kitchen as Emma left.

'I think I'll go now,' he told Miss Millie. 'Thanks very much for inviting me to dinner — that and the music have helped a lot.'

He looked at Emma. 'Tell Bill that I will walk home with you when it's time — just give me a knock,' he said. 'Gran and Grandad are staying with Mum. It gives them time to talk.'

'I'm glad you're coming, Cecil,' said Emma. 'Tell your Mum — we feel very sad for you all.'

'I will, Em — thanks,' he said and went out of the back door as Mum and Jonty came in at the front.

'Settle yourselves down,' said Miss Winnie. 'We'll make a cup of tea.' The two Misses Noble and Mr Noble left the room.

Mum turned anxiously to Emma and Fran. 'How's it been?' she asked.

'About the same,' said Emma, 'but we've tried to think about today. We've made a calendar and just cross off each day as it starts with a red crayon. Makes the week feel shorter.'

'My poor pet, you shouldn't have to be wishing days and weeks away like that,' said Mum anxiously.

'Don't worry Mum,' said Emma. 'We'll survive. Tell us about you, Jonty — and Dad.'

Mum told her how they had moved across and were happily settled with Mrs Smith, who seemed to be a very nice, quiet lady. They talked in the evenings when Jonty was in bed and found they had a lot of things in common.

'What about Dad?' asked Bill. 'Did you talk to him again?'

'Yes, on Tuesday,' replied Mum. 'He rang my telephone box. Next Wednesday I'll ring his, because I haven't been able to give him a number here yet.'

'It's great you can actually talk to Dad,' said Emma, 'even though he's so far away.'

There was a little tap at the door and Miss Millie poked her head round.

'Would Fran and Jonty like to play bagatelle?' she asked.

'Oh yes,' said Fran enthusiastically.

'Goody,' said Jonty. 'I love bagatelle.'

Miss Millie put the board on the floor and gave them five marbles and a stick.

'There you are,' she said. 'We'll be in later with a cup of tea.'

As she closed the door, Mum said, 'One very exciting thing Dad told me. His boss's wife and children are in Reading and he *might* be coming up to see them.'

'Would he be able to bring Dad?' asked Emma eagerly.

'Well — he's half promised,' replied Mum. 'The trouble is — petrol. You know, it's rationed and somehow, he's got to be able to get enough.'

'What about the black market?' asked Bill.

'Bill — how could you?' said Mum, reproachfully, but with a little smile.

'Well,' said Bill, 'I don't usually believe in cheating and things — but we're a good cause, aren't we?'

'Be lovely to see Dad,' said Emma, with a deep sigh.

'He even said, that if the invasion doesn't happen in a few weeks, the boss is going to take his wife and children home.' Mum told them.

'Would he take us home too?' Bill asked hopefully.

'I *think* Dad might ask him to take Jonty and me,' said

Mum. 'Then you all come home by train at the end of term.'

'In time for Christmas,' said Emma.

'Christmas,' put in Fran, 'that's not for *ages*.'

'It'll soon be here, duck,' Mum assured her. 'The leaves are turning brown and coming off the trees.'

'I've *never* wanted Christmas so badly as I want it this year,' said Emma glumly.

'If the invasion happens — none of us will be able to go,' Mum warned them.

'I shall pray every night for God to stop it,' said Emma intensely.

'We'll all do that, love,' said Mum. 'And I think our airmen are doing their best.'

Chapter Twenty-one

GOOD NEWS — OR BAD NEWS?

EMMA and Fran could hardly wait for news that Dad was coming to Reading. The following week, Mum told them that there was no invasion — but no immediate visit, because the boss could not get enough petrol. They all kept waiting — and hoping.

Time passed slowly. Regular sandwiches and orange squash made boring suppers, but broken biscuits in bed stopped them from feeling hungry. Under pressure from Miss Pring, Emma was able to say —

'How-w — Now-w

Brow-wn — Cow-w'

— and was accused of 'talking posh' by Bill.

Saturdays, they enjoyed with other evacuees in the park, or church hall — and Sundays! Sundays were the high-light of the week. Emma dreaded to think what life would have been like without those lovely Sundays at the Nobles with Mum and the boys.

Sadly, there was still no news of Cecil's father. His mother was being very brave, but she found it hard not knowing whether he was dead or alive. Everyone kept praying that another telegram would come to tell them that he had been picked up by another ship.

The weather had turned cold and Emma was glad of the gloves Miss Millie had given her — not only could she wear her raincoat without being afraid of seeing Duch, but they also kept her hands warm.

It was a wet, windy Sunday and they were glad to reach the warmth of the Nobles' house. A fire was burning in the front room and the living room.

'What a treat,' thought Emma. 'We only have two fires at Christmas.'

Mum was there to have dinner with them, which was a little unusual, because she normally came in the afternoon for tea. Emma and Fran were so delighted to see her and Jonty, that they did not question why she was there.

After the usual lovely Sunday roast dinner, with Yorkshire puddings and plenty of vegetables, Mr Noble said, 'Right — the Nobles are washing up and preparing tea. The Barts are going into the front room to talk.

'I'd like to help,' protested Emma.

'I know you would, m'dear,' said Mr Noble, 'but not today.'

He patted her on the shoulder and gently ushered her into the front room. Soon, they were all sitting down and Emma began wondering what all this was about. It was not quite normal!

Mum was looking serious. 'I'm not quite sure where to begin,' she said. 'Things are happening so quickly.'

'What sort of things?' asked Emma in a worried voice.

'Nothing bad,' smiled Mum. 'When I spoke to Dad on the phone this week, he said that his boss had managed, at last, to get enough petrol to come to Reading.'

'Goody,' said Fran. 'Is he bringing Dad?'

'Well, no,' said Mum. 'That's the point. It took him so long to save up enough petrol coupons, that he's afraid he won't be able to do it again before Christmas.'

'So what's he going to do then?' asked Bill.

'He's coming up to Reading today, staying the night, then taking his wife and children back tomorrow.' Mum explained. She paused and looked at their faces to see if they had guessed what she was going to say next.

Excitement had faded away and their worried eyes asked the questions that their mouths did not want to speak.

'Dad would like me to go back with them,' Mum said quietly. 'The invasion scare is over.'

'Oh Mum, are we going to lose you?' Emma sounded desperate. She felt as if her whole world was falling apart. *Nothing*, absolutely *nothing*, was secure any more.

Mum put her arm round her and said gently, 'Listen love, this really is a good sign. I can go back — Dad says it's safe — then you can come home in time for Christmas.'

'Can we really, Mum?' asked Bill.

'I promise,' said Mum. 'If it's safe for me and Jonty, then I'm sure it will be safe for all of you.'

'How will *we* get back?' asked Emma doubtfully.

'Dad's been talking to Mr King about that,' Mum told them. 'It's all going to be arranged between Mr King and Miss Cannon. He thinks that quite a lot of people will want to go home by Christmas, now that there's not going to be an invasion.'

'I trust Mr King,' said Bill. 'I might be a bit afraid of him, but he's O.K. If he promises something — it'll happen.'

'Even Miss Cannon will listen to him,' added Emma, looking a little happier.

'If *only* we were still with Phil and not with that *awful* Mrs Crick,' wailed Fran.

'I know, my pet,' said Mum, trying to comfort her. 'She's

certainly the reason why we want to get you home as soon as possible.'

'What happens now?' asked Bill.

'Dad's boss is coming round this evening, just to make sure everything's all right and to arrange what time we leave in the morning,' replied Mum. 'It will be pretty early, I think, because it's a long way and he doesn't want to go through London, in case there are any air raids.'

'How will Dad know whether you're definitely going?' asked Emma.

'Now, that's the big surprise,' said Mum and smiled broadly. 'At three o'clock, we're all going to be at the phone box. Dad will ring!'

There were squeals of excitement from all four children.

'Can *we* talk to him?' asked Bill, eagerly.

'Just a few words,' said Mum. 'The trouble is, in a phone box money runs out so quickly.'

'At least we'll hear his voice,' said Emma and gave a happy sigh.

'Good-ee,' said Fran.

'Jonty,' said Mum, 'you can wait and talk to Dad at home.' He looked disappointed at not being able to use the phone.

'You're the lucky one,' said Bill. 'You'll have Dad all to yourself and be able to talk to him lots and lots from now until Christmas.'

Jonty's face brightened up, just as there was a little knock at the door and Miss Millie's voice called, 'Can we come in with a cup of tea?'

'Yes do,' said Mum. 'Open the door, Bill.'

He did and Miss Millie came in with a tray of cups and saucers. Miss Winnie followed with the teapot. They both looked anxiously at the Barts.

'Do they know?' asked Miss Millie.

162

'Yes,' said Mum. 'I've told them. They were all a bit shocked at first.'

'We didn't think we were going to lose Mum so soon,' said Emma sadly.

'We understand,' said Miss Millie. 'That's hard — especially as your Mrs Crick is so unkind.'

'Listen, my love,' joined in Miss Winnie. 'Every Sunday, 'til you go home, you can come here and share the day with us.'

'It's my treat of the week,' said old Mr Noble, coming into the room with a plate of biscuits in his hand. 'I love having you two young girls around. Really cheers me up.'

Emma took a deep breath. 'Thank you, thank you so much,' she said. 'I really don't know what we'd do without a proper home to come to on Sundays.'

'Run away,' said Fran glumly.

'Well,' laughed Mr Noble, 'if you run away from the Crick's, make sure you run here!'

Mum gave him a thankful look. She was obviously very worried about what was happening to Emma and Fran — and so thankful that Bill was with nice people who were not only happy to care for him, but watch over the girls too.

Emma looked at the clock — quarter to three.

'Is it time to go and talk to Dad?' she asked eagerly.

'I think so,' said Mum. 'By the time we get our coats on and across to the phone box, Dad will be ringing.'

Chapter Twenty-two

GOODBYE MUM

WHEN they reached the red phone box at the end of the road, somebody else was already in it. Anxiously, they waited outside, looking at their watches.

'What happens if it's three o'clock and that man is still in there?' asked Emma. 'Will Dad speak to him?'

'No,' said Mum. 'Dad will get a funny sound on his phone to tell him that someone else is using this phone, so he'll have to keep trying.'

'Has it happened before?' asked Bill.

'Well once,' Mum told them. 'I was waiting and waiting and the phone didn't ring. I thought Dad had forgotten — or I'd got the wrong time.'

'Then what?' asked Bill.

'At last it rang,' said Mum 'and Dad told me that someone else had been in *his* phone box and he had to wait for ages for them to come out.'

'I s'pose everybody's trying to use phones to talk these days,' said Emma. 'There are so many people away from home — either in the Forces, or evacuated. Everyone's worried about their families.'

'Yes,' agreed Mum, 'and not many ordinary people have got telephones in their own house.'

'P'raps they will be able to after the war,' said Bill. 'At least we all know how jolly useful phones are. We didn't before.'

The phone box door was pushed open and a man stepped out.

'Sorry to keep you waiting,' he said. 'Just phoning my son. He's in the Air Force. Making sure he's O.K., you know.'

'Is he?' asked Mum.

'Yes, thank God,' said the man. 'He's a gunner and keeps flying in these air battles. I don't like it. Frightening.' The man shook his head.

They all understood how he felt. They had *seen* those air battles and watched what happened to the planes.

'How awful to look up thinking that someone you know might be up there,' thought Emma. She had a mental picture of those planes zooming out of the sky with smoke pouring from their tails. She shuddered.

The phone began ringing and Mum rushed into the box.

'Quick,' she said. 'Pile in.' They did — or rather, squashed in. Mum lifted the receiver.

'Hello,' she said, rather nervously. 'Reading 3692.'

They waited breathlessly.

Then — 'Hello,' she said again and this time, sounded as if she meant it.

'Yes. I've got them all here,' she said. 'Bit of a squash.' She laughed . . .

. . . 'Yes, I've told them.' . . .

. . . 'Well, they can't wait to come too, especially the girls.' . . .

'Yes — here they are. Say hello to Dad.' Mum handed the phone to Bill.

'Hello,' he said cautiously. Then his face broke into a

smile as he heard Dad. After a few words, he said 'goodbye' and handed it on to Emma.

'Hello,' said Emma, not sure what was going to happen next.

'Hang on,' said Dad's voice and she heard clung, clung, clung at the other end.

'That's better,' he said. 'I've put some more money in, so that we won't be cut off. Is that you Emma?'

'Oh yes Dad. Lovely to hear you. Can't wait for Christmas.'

'Neither can I,' said Dad. 'I'm longing to see you all. But at least Mum'll be here to get the food ready — otherwise it would be spuds, spuds and more spuds.'

Emma giggled.

'Fran's turn,' Mum whispered .

'Bye Dad,' said Emma into the phone and handed it on to Fran, who was so excited, she could hardly talk — then she started and didn't want to stop!

Mum said, 'My turn, pet.'

'Bye,' said Fran.

'We're leaving early tomorrow morning,' Mum said, into the phone. 'Not sure how long it will take, but it'll be marvellous to see you again — so soon too. Oh — there are the pips. Bye,' she said and held the phone down.

'Bye,' said Dad's voice.

'Bye,' they chorused — and then he was gone. A burring sound was all that came out of the phone. They tumbled out of the red box onto the pavement. Another family was waiting to squeeze in.

'A miracle,' said Bill. 'Fancy us being able to talk to Dad.'

'And he's all those miles away,' said Emma. She felt happier now that she had actually spoken to him.

'What were you giggling about?' asked Bill and she told him what Dad had said about nothing to eat but potatoes.

They all laughed and felt happier for it. As they reached the Nobles, a telegram boy pulled up on his bike beside them. They stood and looked to see where he would go. In his trim navy uniform and little cap, he went to Cecil's door and knocked. Quickly, Mum steered them to the Noble's door and knocked.

Mr Noble opened it. As they stepped inside, Mum said, 'The telegram boy has just gone next door. I didn't want us all to be in the road watching, in case it's bad news.'

'We saw,' said Mr Noble quietly. 'Let's hope. They'll

come and tell us.' He turned to the children. 'How's Dad?' he asked. 'Was he pleased to hear you?'

'Great,' said Bill. 'Marvellous to talk to him.'

'Come and tell me all about it,' called Miss Winnie from the front room.

They all started talking at once, with Miss Winnie, Miss Millie and Mr Noble sharing their excitement. Suddenly, the front room door burst open and Cecil stood there.

'They've found him. They've found him,' he shouted, hardly able to contain himself, he was so happy.

'Sorry to burst in,' he said, suddenly realising what he'd done, 'but I had to tell someone!'

'Where have they found him?' asked Mr Noble. They were all feeling thrilled for Cecil and his mother.

'An American boat picked him up and he's now in the United States,' Cecil told them. 'I don't s'pose he'll get back for ages, 'cos he's got some injuries. But at least — we know he's alive.'

'We're thrilled,' said Miss Winnie. 'Where's your Mum? I bet she's feeling so happy.'

'She's just getting her hat and coat on to go and tell Gran and Grandad. I'm walking round with her, so mustn't stop,' said Cecil. 'Bye' — and he rushed out almost as quickly as he came in.

'What a relief,' said Mum.

'Even if he doesn't get home for a few months,' said Mr Noble, 'at least they know he's going to come back — one day.'

'Hope the injuries are not too severe,' said Miss Winnie thoughtfully.

'But at least in America, they've good hospitals and they're not at war, so they haven't got the problems we have,' added Miss Millie.

'How *will* he get home?' asked Bill.

'Well, probably on a cargo boat — Merchant Navy, or something.' Mr Noble explained. 'The Americans will organise it.'

Emma was very quiet throughout Sunday tea. Everything was delicious — the scones, the home-made jam and beautiful sponge cake. But, she was aware that this was to be the last meal they were to share with Mum for a long time. It was a bit like the last breakfast at home before they evacuated. The others seemed to be talking normally and Mum kept giving her little worried looks.

When they had finished, Miss Winnie asked, 'Are you going to walk home with the girls Bill?'

'Course,' said Bill. 'Won't have Cecil with us today.'

'I'll come to the end of the road with you,' said Mum. Then, turning to the Miss Nobles, she said, 'I'll come back and help with the washing up. Feeling a bit guilty. Haven't done anything today — and you're so good to us all.'

'That's all right, m'dear,' said Miss Winnie. 'It's our pleasure to help. We're not suffering much from the war ourselves, so the least we can do is to help those who are.'

The girls got ready to go and said 'goodbye' to the Nobles.

'See you next week,' said Mr Noble. 'I'll look forward to that.'

'So will we,' said Miss Millie and Miss Winnie.

They walked to the end of the road, saying very little. Emma could not trust herself to speak and, the closer she got to saying goodbye to Mum, the worse she felt. At the corner, Mum hugged and kissed them both.

'I'll be thinking about you,' she said gently, 'and I promise that Dad and I will bring you home as soon as we possibly can.'

'I know, Mum,' said Emma, struggling with the tears.

'Be brave, my pet,' said Mum. She gave them another hug and then said to Bill, 'Look after them. I'll see you when you get back.'

They waved, turned the corner and were on their way back to the Cricks for another week of misery.

Chapter Twenty-three

LEAVING — AT LAST!

THE weeks dragged by. The weather got colder. Their bedroom at the Crick's felt icy and they spent many evenings shivering under the eiderdown, until one evening, Mr Crick brought up a little paraffin oil stove.

'I think you're going to need this,' he said, carrying it into their room. 'I'll come up and light it for you when I get home from work. It's too dangerous for you to light yourselves.' He showed Emma how to turn it off when they went to bed.

Before he left them, he said in a very quiet voice, 'My wife's not very happy about having an oil stove up here. She says it will make the room smell horrid. I agree — it will, but,' he said firmly, 'I told her it was either the oil stove, or you coming downstairs in the evening to share our fire. That did it! You've got the oil stove.'

He gave a little grin and left the room.

'Well,' whispered Emma as he left, 'he's braver than you think.'

'He does *really* care about us, doesn't he?' said Fran.

'Yes, he does,' agreed Emma. 'It's only her. Let's have some broken biscuits.'

Pat always managed to 'find' a halfpenny in her pocket

once a week, so that they could buy a new supply. Because Dad had to pay money for their food and everything whilst they were evacuated, there did not seem to be any left over for pocket money — even a penny a week. Mum had explained all of this whilst she was in Reading. Emma wondered if that was one of the reasons Mum was going home —it cost too much for them all to be away.

Both she and Fran were very thankful that Pat managed to 'find' a halfpenny in her pocket every week. She murmured about her mother 'knowing Mrs Crick — and being sorry.'

After a particularly bad speech training session with Miss Pring, Emma was asked to stay behind. Peggy pulled a face, but could not say anything, because Pring's sharp ears would have picked up the Kentish tones.

'Emma Barton,' said Miss Pring, as the other girls left. 'Miss Cannon would like to see you now in her study. Follow me.'

A very worried Emma followed her down the corridors.

'What have I done?' she thought. 'What's happened now?' she puzzled and puzzled until they reached the study door. Miss Pring knocked.

'Come in,' called the voice. Miss Pring went in.

'Emma Barton to see you, Miss Cannon,' she said, and ushered Emma in, then went out, firmly closing the door behind her.

'Thank goodness she's gone,' thought Emma. 'Would have been worse with both of them here.'

Miss Cannon looked up from her papers.

'Good afternoon, Emma,' she said.

'Good afternoon, Miss Cannon,' said Emma.

'Mr King has been in touch with me about you going home,' continued Miss Cannon and Emma's spirits began to lift. 'He suggests that your brother, your younger sister and you, return with me on Saturday, as I am already escorting another family back.'

'This Saturday!' exclaimed Emma, hardly able to grasp the good news. It was Thursday today!

'Yes — this Saturday,' repeated Miss Cannon. 'I have spoken to your brother's headmaster and have written to your host and hostess, Mr and Mrs Crick. Will you take the letter home with you today, please?'

'Ye–es,' said Emma enthusiastically, just longing to hand over that letter to Mrs Crick. Leaving — at last!

'On Saturday morning,' went on Miss Cannon, 'I will meet you at Reading station at nine o'clock to catch the nine-fifteen train. We *should* then be home by tea-time, unless there are delays.'

'Does Dad know?' asked Emma.

'Mr King has informed your parents and your father will meet you at the West Station,' Miss Cannon replied. 'How will you get to Reading station?'

'I don't know yet,' said Emma, 'but we'll find a way,' she ended with a smile.

'Perhaps your host, or hostess, will take you?' suggested Miss Cannon.

'Our hostess certainly won't take us and I'm sure that she will not allow our host to,' said Emma grimly.

'You sound very sure?' Miss Cannon seemed surprised.

'I *am* sure,' said Emma. 'Thank you Miss Cannon for this good news. We will look forward to going home with you on Saturday.'

'Thank you, Emma,' said Miss Cannon. 'You may return to your class.'

Emma felt as if she was walking on air, as she went back along the corridors, the precious letter to the Crick's held firmly in her hand. Just two more nights and they would be on their way home! It was hard to believe that the nightmare was nearly over.

She opened the classroom door to find a Maths lesson in progress. Miss Plath turned as she went in.

'Sit down, Emma,' she said with a smile, 'and try to catch up with what we're doing.'

The bell rang shortly afterwards and Miss Plath called her to the front.

'I think you've had good news,' she said.

Emma beamed. 'Marvellous news,' she said. 'We're going home on Saturday.'

'I'm glad for you,' said Miss Plath with a warm smile, as she left the room.

The other girls crowded round and Emma shared her excitement with them. There were some envious looks, as if they would all like to be catching the train home on Saturday morning.

Eventually, the final bell rang and Emma ran off to find Mary and Fran. As soon as she saw them she burst out, 'We're going home.'

'When?' asked the surprised Mary.

'Saturday,' Emma told her with delight.

'Sat–ur–day — home,' said Fran in wonder.

'You lucky things,' said Mary, as they linked up with Pat and Annie.

On the way home, Emma told them all about her interview with Miss Cannon.

'Strange,' she thought. 'I shall miss them all — our walks home together.'

When they reached the end of the path and were on the road, she had a sudden idea.

'I think I'd like to call on Phil,' she said, 'just to let her know — and say "goodbye".'

They reached the white gate and Emma and Fran left

the others. Going up to Phil's front door Emma knocked — and they waited. The door opened. Phil was surprised and delighted to see them.

'Come in — come in,' she said. 'Let's have a cup of tea.'

Following her into the kitchen, they felt quite at home, and sat down at the table to share their excitement with her. Emma went on to tell her how unhappy they'd been with Mrs Crick and how much they'd missed staying with her.

'You poor lambs,' said Phil sympathetically. 'I'm glad you're going home to your Mum and Dad.'

There was a knock at the door and when Phil opened it, they heard Charlie's voice.

'Great,' he said. 'I'm glad to see them again.'

He came into the kitchen with a broad smile on his face.

'Good news. I hear,' he said. 'No invasion — so "goodbye Reading!" I'm very glad for you. How are you getting to the station on Saturday with those cases?'

'Not sure really,' said Emma.

'Will those Cricks take you? asked Charlie.

'No I'm sure they won't,' said Emma firmly. 'They're not that nice — at least, *she's* not — and he's afraid of her.'

'Tell you what,' said Charlie, 'I'll take you in the car.'

'Will you?' Emma was delighted. She had never even thought of that.

'And I'll come too,' said Phil, 'to give you a good send off.'

'Thank you — thank you,' said Emma.

'Great,' said Fran.

'Pick you up at half past eight on Saturday morning,' said Charlie. 'Whereabouts?'

Emma gave Phil the address and she wrote it down.

'I think we'd better go,' she said. 'Mrs Crick doesn't know yet. I've got a letter for her from my headmistress.'

They went to the door and Phil and Charlie waved them off.

'See you Saturday,' said Phil.

'Perfect,' thought Emma. 'What a perfect way to begin the journey home.'

At last they reached the Crick's house. When they knocked, there was no reply, so Emma found her key and they went in. In their room, they started to pack.

'Why not?' said Emma. 'It'll make us feel that we're really going.'

Soon, all of their clothes were spread out on the bed, ready to put into their empty cases. This took a long time and they laughed and chatted as they did it. For the first time in this room, they felt happy.

'Haven't heard Madam Crick come in,' said Emma. It was quite dark outside and usually, she was home with Shirley before this.

'Not bothered,' said Fran — and they got on with their packing.

A long time later, they heard the front door open and footsteps go through into the kitchen, then return along the hall and up the stairs.

There was a knock at the bedroom door and Mr Crick's voice called out, 'Would you like to come down and have some supper?'

Emma and Fran looked at each other in surprise and went to open the door.

'My wife's not coming home tonight,' he said, looking a bit agitated. 'I've brought in some fish and chips. Would you like to come down and share them with me?'

'Yes please, Mr Crick,' said Emma eagerly and they followed him downstairs.

It was the nicest meal that they had had in the Crick's house. The fish and chips tasted really good and they certainly did not feel hungry when they'd finished. Mr Crick was very friendly — but did not say why his wife was away, nor for how long.

As they finished, Emma fumbled in her pocket and handed him Miss Cannon's letter.

'My headmistress asked me to give you this,' she said and watched his face as he read it.

'I'm sure that you'll both be very pleased to get back home to your parents,' he said finally. 'I hope — I hope that you've not been too unhappy here,' he finished awkwardly.

'Oh no — Oh no,' said Emma hurriedly. What else *could* she say?

'I'm not sure whether my wife will come home tomorrow,' he said. 'If she doesn't, will fish and chips be all right again?'

'Oh yes — lovely,' said Emma.

'How will you get to the station on Saturday?' Mr Crick asked suddenly.

'Some friends are taking us in their car,' replied Emma, *very* relieved that she had an answer ready.

Mr Crick looked equally relieved. 'I'm glad,' he said. 'Very glad.'

Chapter Twenty-four

HELLO DAD

HALF past eight on Saturday morning arrived. There was a knock at the door and Mr Crick went to answer it.

'It's Charlie,' whispered Emma to Fran, as they stood in the kitchen all ready to go.

'Morning,' they heard Charlie say.

'Good morning,' said Mr Crick. 'It is really very kind of you to take the girls to the station.'

'My pleasure,' said Charlie. 'Are their cases ready?'

'Here they are,' said Mr Crick and handed the cases to Charlie. Emma and Fran came to join them at the front door.

'Goodbye. Have a safe journey,' said Mr Crick and held out his hand first to Emma and then to Fran. *'I've* enjoyed having you.'

'Thank you, Mr Crick,' said Emma. 'Give our love to Shirley.' No-one mentioned Mrs Crick.

The girls walked down to Phil, Charlie and the waiting car. Mr Crick stood alone on the doorstep waving goodbye to them.

'Wonder what'll happen to him now?' thought Emma and felt really sorry for him.

Fran was bouncing happily up and down on the seat beside her.

'Excited about going home?' Phil asked her.

'Oh yes,' said Fran. 'It'll be love-ly to see Dad, Mum and Jonty again.'

Charlie drove through the streets and pulled up outside Reading station. Bill and the Nobles were already there.

'Had to come and say goodbye m'dears,' said old Mr Noble as the girls climbed out of Charlie's car. He bent down and gave them both a kiss.

'It's been so nice having you to share our Sundays.'

Miss Winnie and Miss Millie kissed them too.

'If you ever come to Reading — even when you're grown-up — please come over and see us,' said Miss Winnie.

'Bill has promised to,' said Miss Millie.

'We will — we will,' said Emma enthusiastically.

Then, Miss Cannon arrived.

'Good morning, Emma,' she said. 'I'm glad to meet your brother and sister. You had better say goodbye to your hosts and hostesses, so that we can go through onto the platform.'

There were hugs and kisses from Phil and handshakes from Charlie. Waving goodbye, the Barts followed Miss Cannon through the entrance to the platforms. Emma felt sad as she gave her last wave to that friendly group of adults. *They* were the group of people who had made her and Fran feel happy in Reading. Something within her was glad that she had not been required to say goodbye to Mrs Crick.

Once on the platform, Miss Cannon led the way along to where another boy and girl were standing.

'It's Audrey,' exclaimed Emma.

'Yes,' said Bill. 'Didn't have a chance to tell you that

Tommy and his sister were going home at the same time.'

'Oh,' said Miss Cannon. 'I'm glad you all know each other. That will make the journey easier.'

Emma was delighted. She had been wondering how they were going to pass the time talking only to Miss Cannon.

With a lot of noise and steam the train approached.

'Stand back! Stand back!' shouted the porter and they did as they were told. He waited by their group as the train puffed to a stop. He opened a carriage door, picked up some of the cases and led the way into a compartment. Between them, they followed with the rest of the baggage. Miss Cannon tipped him as he left and they heard the carriage door slam.

Lots of doors slammed and the guard's whistle blew. The train steamed out of Reading station and Emma sighed contentedly. They were on their way home.

No-one spoke until the town with the biscuit factory was behind them. Then, Miss Cannon opened her bag and produced some packs of cards.

'I thought the girls might like to play Happy Families with Fran — and the boys could use the playing cards,' she said. 'It will make the time pass more quickly and I have some work to do.'

Certainly the time did pass quickly and the games were quietly enjoyed as the train rumbled towards London. They reached the outskirts and stopped looking at their cards, as they watched for bombed buildings.

'Has there been more bombing on London?' Tommy asked Miss Cannon.

'I'm afraid so,' she replied. 'Each time I go on this journey, I see more and more damage. It is really very sad.'

'There hasn't been any bombing at home, has there?' asked Audrey anxiously.

'No. There hasn't,' replied Miss Cannon.

'We haven't any factories and things,' said Bill, 'that they'd want to hit.'

'The most important thing is the cathedral,' said Emma.

'No point in bombing that,' said Audrey. 'That's not going to make much difference to winning or losing the war.'

'No,' said Miss Cannon with confidence. 'Now that the invasion threat is over, I think that we shall be quite safe in our city. Now, have you got your sandwiches to eat?'

'Oh yes,' said Audrey and Tommy.

'Oh no,' said Emma. She had not thought of those — and certainly Mr Crick hadn't either.

'It's O.K.,' said Bill. 'The Nobles have given me sandwiches for you two. They didn't think Mrs Crick would give you any.'

'But weren't they the Cricks who brought you to the station?' asked a puzzled Miss Cannon. 'They seemed very nice people.'

'Oh no. They weren't the Cricks,' explained Emma, feeling embarrassed. 'That was the lady we were taken away from. She was very nice — and so was her friend with the car.'

'I see,' said Miss Cannon slowly, still looking puzzled. Fortunately, she did not ask any more questions.

'Just as well,' thought Emma. 'I don't know how I would have explained about Mrs Crick's disappearance. It's all over now,' she reminded herself. 'I don't have to think about her ever again.'

She and Fran enjoyed the Noble's sandwiches and they all munched away as the train rumbled through London. It was a dull, grey December day outside, but *inside* the compartment, Emma was feeling anything but dull and grey. These had been her feelings on the outward journey, when she was going into nothingness.

Now, she imagined Mum preparing supper and Dad getting on his bike once again to ride to the West Station to meet them.

The buildings of London disappeared. There had been no sirens and no train hold-ups. Soon the ploughed fields and the bare orchards of Kent could be seen. The sky began to darken and Emma knew that they would not reach home in the daylight.

She imagined the walk home from the station, through the Westgate Towers, along the High Steet, Beer Cart Lane and Castle Street towards the Norman Castle, Winfield — and home.

It would be quite pitch dark. In the blackout, no lights would shine out from street lamps, or houses, but Emma would not need the lights to show her legs the way to go home. They would happily find their way without instructions from her eyes. Her thoughts drifted on.

Miss Cannon's voice brought her back into the railway compartment.

'We're nearly there,' she said. 'Put your coats on — and boys, get the cases down.'

Soon they were ready, just waiting for the train to slow up and pull into the station. In the darkness, the shapes of buildings could be seen against the sky. A tall tower, rising above everthing else, gave Emma a thrill.

'The cathedral!' she thought. 'We really are back home.'

The train rumbled over the level crossing, behind the houses in Station Road and into the West Station. She could hardly contain her excitement.

'Back,' she thought. 'Back home.'

How different were her feelings from those four months ago, when the train was taking her away from the city.

With puffs of smoke and squeals from the brakes, the train halted in the station. They bundled out onto the dark platform, picked up their cases, went down the steps, under the subway — and emerged into the tiny, dim light of the ticket collector's box.

Peeping over the shoulder of the ticket collector was a face — a man with black hair and a black moustache. A flat cap was on his head and a scarf wrapped around his neck.

It was Dad.

'Oh Dad,' cried Emma, as she rushed through the doorway into his arms.

They were home. Evacuation was over.